ICONic

great, awesome, best.

*'Have an **ICONic** day.'*

U*RBAN* ***D****ICTIONARY*

Stoned Crows
& other Australian icons

prose poetry and
microfiction

edited by
Julie Chevalier & Linda Godfrey

SPINELESS WONDERS

www.shortaustralianstories.com.au

Spineless Wonders

BN01164417

PO Box 220

STRAWBERRY HILLS

New South Wales, Australia, 2012

www.shortaustralianstories.com.au

First published by Spineless Wonders 2013

Cover image and book design by Bettina Kaiser

www.bettinakaiser.com.

Copyediting and layout by Bronwyn Mehan.

Typeset in Bodoni MT

Printed and bound by Lightning Source Australia

ISBN 978-0-9874479-0-6

For

Bev Mehan

& her iconic beach house, Fingal Bay

Contents

Introduction

I lost my sock in the Laundromat of laugh—Mark O'Fynn

First came Vivienne Plumb's generous suggestion that Spineless Wonders publish an anthology riffing off her collection of prose poems, Cheese and onion sandwiches and other New Zealand icons (Seraph Press, 2011). It was easy to assemble a humongous list of Aussie icons but they looked ready for retirement. Carol Jenkins suggested we look for 'clever small pieces that take a sideways shove at new and yet-to-be discovered' icons as well as the old ones. 'A leap of imagination and de-cliché-isation. Pieces that take a self-critical look at Australian life.'

We mentioned two artworks from the collection at the Art Gallery New South Wales to illustrate how visual artists had successfully reinterpreted Aussie icons. If you haven't seen the art works, you've probably seen the postcards. Polychromed wooden bats hang from a Hills Hoist in Lin Onus's fibreglass sculpture, Fruit Bats, 1991. An Opera House of white china plates is stacked against an upended teacup in a dish rack in Eric Thanke's linocut, An Opera House in every home (1972). That was the sort of idea we were looking for.

Reader, we could never have predicted that Margaret Olley, Ben Quilty, Brett Whitely, an underground madman named

Axel and a disturbing father at Sculpture by the Sea, would have ear worms, see dolphins in wet suits, judge cake competitions at Ag Shows, suffer travel anxiety, camp with crocs, go to Byron Bay, Luna Park, Central, Surry Heights, and Bunnings. Who would guess that kind bus drivers would veer off the route to take migrants crafting toy kangaroos and jewellery boxes in fluffy slippers, and school boys wearing Stamina trousers, to beaches? We find joggers who witnessed the collapse of HIH, the corporate coal face and coal seam mining while enjoying fries, sundaes, lamingtons and custard. As road trains barrel up open highways flirting with Donald Sutherland, parts of our national broadcaster are being sold off to dictatorships and laminated signs, stuck on the walls of office buildings, prescribe the rules of engagement. Who knew there was nostalgia for the tram depot to return to Bennelong Point? Or that the Opera House would transform into an operating theatre?

The Editorial Team had to retreat to Bev's Beach House to savour such a feast (along with prawns, mussels, wine, laughter and swims.)

'Like getting a love letter,' Bron Mehan said as she read out Peter Lach-Newinsky's Iconostasis.

Bron is the driving force of Spineless Wonders and we again thank her for her energy, sense of fun, expertise, hard work and vision.

Julie Chevalier & Linda Godfrey

Editors, 2013

Letter from New Zealand

The idea of encouraging writers to pen a poem that uses the subject of an Australian iconic object came from a serendipitous meeting between myself, Bronwyn Mehan and Julie Chevalier, after I showed them my collection of thirty-nine prose poems that use New Zealand 'iconic' subjects (The Cheese and Onion Sandwich and Other New Zealand Icons, Seraph Press, Wellington, 2011). This small collection has proven to be popular in New Zealand.

Pondering one day on how to encourage more readers to poetry (poetry is often assumed to be 'difficult' to read), I hit on the idea of using nationally popular subjects, such as the infamous Kiwi cheese and onion sandwich, a more unusual sammy filling that I first encountered when I travelled to New Zealand many moons ago (my mother was a Kiwi, my father an Australian).

The prose poem details the story of my original experience with this sandwich at the Golden Crust Café, Dunedin, where I was served by a woman by the name of Valmai. I embraced the cheese and onion, and this led me to develop a deeper understanding of exactly how it must be prepared—no large chunks of onion, please! Other iconic subject matter in the collection includes severe weather warnings (everpresent in New Zealand), whitebait, the tangi (Maori funeral rites now adopted by some Pakeha), the ferry crossing between the north and the south islands, Crown Lynn china, and motels in Taupo.

Some pieces are tinged with a tiny political bite: 'bluestone kerbing' outlines the disappearance of the old aesthetically-pleasing bluestone kerbing blocks from the poorer Auckland suburbs. Suspiciously, broken or damaged bluestone kerbstones are always able to be replaced with 'spare' old blocks in the more fashionable, richer areas. 'Bargains' was another Kiwi subject. The Pakeha/Scottish background has always meant that a 'bargain' has been popular in New Zealand, where I have even heard the saying: *it is bad luck to walk past a garage sale.*

What makes something iconic? Originally, an icon was an image or representation that was regarded as being holy or sacred. To describe something as iconic has changed in meaning somewhat and is now defined as something 'well known or famous' that is 'representative of a particular idea'. For instance, the cheese and onion sandwich can be defined as being well known in New Zealand, and represents a particular kind of nostalgia that relates to the 'old' days, the days when a spade was a spade, and so forth. The cheese and onion sandwich is a sort of 'Kiwiana' food, like lamingtons, chocolate fish, and scones and porridge. Iconic subject matter is really just good old-fashioned symbols, pointing and pastiching their way towards emotions of nationality and identity.

On the other hand, an icon is an icon is an icon. What may seem symbolic to me may not be so important to my neighbour. We all have our own opinions of what feels iconic and I think that writers will have had fun defining their particular Australian icons.

Vivienne Plumb
Auckland, 2013

11

Peter Lach-Newinsky

iconostasis

first door: god's eye webcam

toyota samsung miele ge maccas all sitting together in their
second life on a screen in a gaming den in seoul chewing kimchi
with roo & a fair shake of the sauce bottle as the webcam scans
in over the opera house mumbling NO WAR in a laconic sort
of way iphoned out to all the second gen boat people selling
smack out west to seventh gen boat people lebs & serbs wearing
maori tats on their harleys like hopper on speed or hogan on
tim tams as the st johns st pauls st andrews sandstone bogans
prepare for their laidback lawyer lives in mosman woollahra
cayman islands & the odd pole-dancer taken to a long lunch at
the emirates marquee in a pavlova fascinator stumbles her 20
inch stilettos over the dropped vc of the latest warrior & mate to
come home in a flag with a 21 gun salute for the lanky governor
mate in canary yellow always good for going down mines before
they collapse like the oz top order or collateral debt obligations
to keep the home air cons burning the sun setting in the west
as it still does but who knows for how long so we might take a
punt on it if we've got a tip or two on the likely moods of the
southern ocean index raising a dust storm in the stock exchange
of our hearts big as phar lap's ghost in the fifth at flemington
hong kong racing round uluru stoned as a schoolie zoned out as
a pokie pensioner cloned as a yank in an akubra made in china

licking a wasabi chiko roll along bondi beach coz it sucks like
harold holt's yellow peril submarine we all live in

second door: glossolalia

visuals: face like a dropped pie head like a chewed mintie useless
as tits on a bull useless as a letterbox on a tombstone couldn't
fight his way out of a wet paper bag couldn't organise a fart in
a curry house if he fell into a barrel full of tits he'd come up
sucking his thumb as popular as a cross-city tunnel wouldn't
shout in a shark attack full as a corby boogie board bag vanished
like a fart in a fan factory

sound check: rain on an iron roof, a creaky gate/an outdoor dunny
door banging in the wind/driving over a cow grate/a screen door
slamming/galahs coming in before sunset/geckos chattering on
a ceiling/splat of a cane toad on bitumen/squeak of a hills hoist/
swipe of a credit card/magpies warbling/yobs screaming fuck off
poofter from their holden commodore/spreading disease with the
greatest of ease /a little each day /is a good recipe/it's time

song: love me drizza, love me kubra/love me sheila, love me
clacka/love me wanka, love me heidegga/love me warnie, love
me horny/love me vb, love me tv/love me reffo, love me biffo/love
me smoko, love me choko/love me porno, love me adorno/love me
ute, love me root

third door: the history biffos trinity

white armband
rum rebellion: officers remove an unsatisfactory governor
eureka stockade: heroic uprising of battlers against unjust
authorities of the time
gallipoli: birth of the nation in the heroic sacrifice of our diggers

13

vietnam: another heroic sacrifice of our diggers in defence of
freedom
lambing flats riots: the what?
cronulla riots: minor tussle over correct female beach attire

black armband
rum rebellion: a section of the officer mafia corners the rum
market
eureka stockade: the volk arises in a rage over mining taxes
gallipoli: the volk scrambles up a faux-trojan crag to kill turks
for the british empire
vietnam: the volk hacks thru faux-coppola jungles killing viet-
namese for us empire
lambing flats riots: the volk rids the gold fields of competing
chinamen
cronulla riots: the flag-wrapped volk bashes beach-staining lebs

grey armband
what: ever
pass: the prawns
what's: the score have a nice

Paul Kew

Saturday night on Jonson Street

'You wanna fresh rhyme?' he asks with a smile,'Byron Bay, land of the free, but not for the likes of you and me...' Saturday night on Jonson Street and I leave the rhyme behind, drift into The Rails, daytime people with their night time faces, Alan the newspaper man whispering into Sally the surgeon's ear, this is why they came to Byron, the dreadlocks and tattoos, all the kiddies escaped from the city, backpackers with BO in yesterday's underwear, you won't see Alan and Sally shaking a leg at Coco's or Cheeky Monkey's, they are locals now, I don't know them and they don't know me...I drift back out, two girls who don't look old enough but are probably already too old come past in their lollipop outfits and tinkerbell lipstick, little narrow hips trying to wiggle and budding breasts trying to bulge, I wonder for a moment if they are already rooting and if they are it doesn't seem right, the boys cruise past in their Commodore, all eyes and alcohol, the p-plates a dead give away, a dire warning, a malignant portent, 'Hey baby!' the girls look up, everybody laughs, the car drives away, a chamber of souls, easy fodder for the angels tonight... into the Northern, a table of first timers bouncing out of their seats as the front bar awakes, their first schooners raised by their first tattoos, looking for girls, looking for action, looking for that story to take back home, they are three hours too early and by then it will be too late, there will

15

always be a bigger tattoo...back on the street the big boy with his guitar is belting out some tunes, another face you never see by day, another mask from the Saturday night wall, maybe thinking about his day job in Ballina, pushing a trolley, scanning your meat, sitting by the river eating a prawn...I cross the road to the next corner, where Jonson Street meets Lawson Street, the centre of town, the centre of the universe, it is here the brothers have staked their claim, they raise their bottles, smiling to me as I walk past, all except the woman with her head between her knees, she is thirty going on a hundred and tonight is just the end of another day...was it her I saw sleeping in the bus shelter this morning as I stalked the streets between downpours, looking for the escape this town has never delivered, except in a rare moment of generosity from the meat manager at Woolies, who I followed as she slapped stickers on chickens and trays of meat and wrote numbers that meant something more to the likes of me...up at the Beachie I have stepped into Aussie heaven, it is like stepping into the cast of Home and Away, everywhere there is skin and schooners, eyes and cigarettes, the band keeps the beat and melody simple and everyone is dancing and no-one is listening and everybody is watching the surfing videos like they have never seen them before...I go into the backroom where the boys are ugly but things more real, slip a fiver into Helen of Troy, 'Don't do it mate,' tattoos of things I've never seen crawl up and down his legs, a grim reaper rising up to his shoulder from some hideous scene below, he takes a swig from a can of Jim Beam and sticks a fag into a toothless grin, I bet ten cents, he bets a dollar twenty five, I wonder where his money is coming from but not where it is going to, my fiver disappearing quickly as Helen and I look blankly at each other, each of us awaiting the other's next move...out in the street I am no richer or wiser, there are people everywhere, something hanging in the air that no-one can grab, like the carnival has just finished and no-one wants to go home, the world is on fire and we are all at loose ends, alone in the night, I decide to head home before one of us explodes... back down Jonson Street, past the divvy vans, a first timer's head pinned to the footpath beneath a bouncer's forearm, a girl screaming in his face, a guy with long hair and a bloody nose slumped against the wall...I make it to the bus stop by the little white church, 'Jesus is not a dirty word', white chairs spread out over the lawn, free pancakes, smiling faces, what would they say if I asked them for a beer, 'Friend, you don't need that here,' friend, I need it everywhere...I climb on the bus, see the driver's friendly face, everyone needs a friend, I just have this face, 'two forty,' he says, I have the right change, once again.

Anna Kerdijk Nicholson

Diurnal—Slurry Heights

junkies, gear in, chatting in our gutter, commuter bikes, suburb framed by Victorian brick and telephone wires, this canvas has bitumen as its gesso, bright graffiti walls bawling tags and in Wimbo Park a wedding dress, tight anorak and Ugg boots, groom carries a bright posy, she flower coronet, bicycle-made-for-two, a border collie on a long tether still chasing and catching her Frisbee, geese perhaps those who chase my dog beaks apart tongues up and out, hissing

Bourke Street Bakery queue, studs nose-rings and tattoos standing chatting, cappuccino moustaches, fennel-and-pork sausage rolls and tomato sauce please, Holy Cow and the Maya curry houses, Langton Centre methodoners and halfway housers, brothels, or Mrs Red & Sons, behind whose scarlet door the smallest elephants in world and sculptures of chilli

The Clock, Bills, Toko bring the suits, inspected by the Man who Walks, where to join The Cycle Lane, back-lane Otto-bin wars, who's a functioning drunk, Yulli's, The Book Kitchen and Kylie Kwong's, when C&D are going to Bhutan, lives of others' cats, where water pools when it rains, how to keep a parking space when the footy's on, when to run inside for cricket score at swelling SCG roar—

the diurnal that won't be grasped or writ.

Tim Heffernan

It always begins at Central

I walk that day seeking the signs carrying in my backpack
Words, trustworthy and true. My letter to the Herald didn't
make the opinion's page but I wasn't surprised as it was poetry,
Today's clouded sky is a gauze bandage to heal this infection.
It always begins at Central and I head down past the sleeping-
bagged cocoons, still grubby and yet to emerge. In George Street
two more are attached by dribbling threads to the steps of St
Peter Julian and the Central Baptist Church. At Saint Andrew's
Cathedral a mural of Jonah and the whale reminds me, I called
to the Lord out of distress and he answered me. So I cross the
road and from the footpath pick up a card, a crossword—the
Gospel truth, All that the Father gives me will come to me. And
at Dymock's I buy some Vonnegut, remembering the first time
I was mad with Revelations and Slaughterhouse 5. At Martin
Place the wreaths from Anzac Day remain clustered around the
Cenotaph and I wonder if I am meant to cry, but there is no
rainbow, only Lawrence begging in his great coat. After I palm
him twenty, we take communion with the Continental Cup-a-
Soup they are giving away. He is a socialist so when he doesn't
finish he hands me his remains and I drink them before we part.
Still thirsting I head to the Mercantile but Duncan's gallery trips
me with Christ amongst the landscapes and for our family's Bible
I choose The Passion because Mel made it look real to me. I take

these things with me to the Quay, only stopping to buy music from the Koories playing there. Climbing the concrete steps the Utzon Room is empty but for a suit coat draped on a chair near the tapestry so I try it on and it fits and I cry out in the Opera House. In the gardens of Farm Cove I pilfer the pockets for answers. Three pens, one a fountain and a message from Anais Nin stitched into the lining, Life shrinks or expands in proportion to one's courage. Inflated, I leave my words at the Art Gallery of NSW and at St Mary's Cathedral I recite my mother's rosary and pray, Make me the channel of your peace. I stop to speak to Lawrence again at the intersection of George Street and Ultimo Road and at Central a silent Jehovah's Witness hands me a pamphlet to read on the train trip home.

jenni nixon

this city

lose yourself in this city of green park beauty sandstone and sparkling glass buildings that grasp the sky of infinite riches and trawl down deprivation alleys where the homeless beg on pavements with cardboard signs and the more enterprising sell copies of the big issue. in this harbour city thumping under constant reconstruction in a bag lady's waltz twirl of traffic through tunnels burning rubber over buried shell middens of the gadigal peoples up on to freeways and down thoroughfares into back alleys in an eternal search for parking. goddess asphalta grant me a place within walking distance that i can take time to get back and forth before ticket inspectors their coffers overflow. this city of red traffic lights stopstart flash headlights on high beam reveal uneven footpaths filled not with gold but pedestrians in a non-stop rush for shop sales and coffee. take a deep breath as bicycle couriers flit out and in before braking screech of tyres and beeping horns in this violent city fuelled by alcohol built on convict sweat and corpses where *eternity* is a prophecy scrawled in chalk. musical fireworks explode on the bridge stitched in steel. as if a statue lovers kiss at the museum of contemporary art as thousands of fruit bats fly over the harbour to the royal botanic gardens flutter high above st vincent's hospice where a dying poet crafts revisions where in taylor square sticky summer heat gays lift their gaze from each other to a flapping sky. the sad face of the full moon slowly climbs over the sydney opera house and everybody is watching reality tv. a transitory manly ferry's foghorn blasts warnings at tourists who scrutinize strange maps upside down in the rocks hear faint sound of bells on warships at anchor before opening doors to trendy stores and quaint pubs the fortune of war hero of waterloo and lord nelson where enfolded history of shanghaied sailors whalers whores and razor gangs enthrall on the ghost walk tour's talk of rats and bubonic plague that led to demolition of thousands of houses and later to green ban protests to save what was left. ibis stalk puddles on concrete in a multibillliondollar playgound at barangaroo. a cocktail of lethal chemicals bleed into busy darling harbour. through pall of grey cloud sydney sprawls dotted with islands netted by rippling water as wooden fingerwharves tease the surge the wash of boats that scythe the bays in bubbles. a giraffe nibbles treetop leaves over at taronga zoo fringed eyelashes blink at the best harbour views in sydney. in this throbbing city driven by corruption and greed another dance an everlasting image etched into memory. the dancing man after the war holding his hat high pirouettes down the years in martin place where soldiers *lest we forget* stand in sad rememberance at the cenotaph. in rowe street once the heart-of-the-city pictureframers printmakers bustling artist's colony now the backend of tall building's ugly laneway *no entry* and *one way* signs above rotting pamphlets cigarette butts syringes used condoms where huddle the homeless who curl into threadbare comfortblankets as shoppingtrolley's spill ecofriendly woolies travelbags. exhale slowly let go this city that never comes to an end

Zoe Annabel Davies

Friday fries and Saturday sundaes

Been here for hours ya know, just sitting, watching the feet. Some girls wear socks with their flat shoes. They have bows on the toes but it looks funny I reckon—nobody wants black feet in black shoes. Other ones have heels that clunk along the footpath, stupid if you think about it. I'm trying to sleep and it's in my ear, real loud. Sometimes I go inside but I get told to get out by the people in the uniforms with those brooms that have dustpans with a handle so you don't have to bend down. I like sundaes but the topping isn't cheap so I get a fifty-cent cone. Used to be twenty cents but maybe they realised it attracted grotty people like me so they put up the price. I get a sundae if someone offers to buy me something instead of giving me money, people do that now more than before. Spend it on drugs anyway, but I'll get a caramel sundae if some stranger's paying. I'm starving hungry some days but I can't always go inside because the weekday workers know my face and the game I play. I'll stand next to the wooden box, you know, the one where they store all the extra salt packets and straws and tissues and stuff—yeah, I hang out there and wait till the girl yells something out. *Large cheeseburger meal with six chicken nuggets and a strawberry thick shake...* If

23

nobody moves I look around. *Large cheeseburger meal with six chicken nuggets and a strawberry thick shake...* She throws the docket on the bench, exasperated and swans off towards the drink machine. Mine. All mine. It's gone before she's back and I'm outta there like a bullet. Smooth as. I give the nuggets to the skinny girl who doesn't talk much. Been hangin' round me like a bad smell all week, must be hungry too. She'll be gone soon for sure. Friday and Saturday nights are the best. Everyone's too drunk to remember ordering and the staff are too pissed off to care about a lost meal or forgotten nuggets. Free food flies and there's half eaten, abandoned food on every surface. I don't know where to start. It's good but I don't feel so flash. That's what life does I guess. Mine's not so bad I guess. I live under the golden arches in Melbourne so can't complain, ey?

Mark O'Flynn

Under the Maw of Luna Park

Jump you fugitive, if you want to escape the fear of fear. Tortoise, rabbit, maybe they are both wrong? Maybe they are each other? From the other side of the synapse I watch a dog watch a cat watch a rat watch a hole from which I am watching understandably out. Think, act, feel, beat with your fists on the floorboards of heaven, cheap timber bought at a discount price, yet immaculately polished. Keep knocking. God ought to make you angry. That's one of his proofs. We did not speak an hour, yet never was so much misunderstood by so many. This is my life, see how I've constructed it, with dreams and dandelions. My father too was a builder of this empty edifice. In the narrow shade a hot man rests. Ask your question stranger. Confusion, doubt, muddle-headedness, welcome back. What's inside that box? Something I made or something I bought? I can't remember. What's outside? Something I found or something I am. Pucker up, cadaver. Let my thoughts be thirsty. Let my old stone starve. Can I lend you some time? Gift wrapped if you like. Repay me when you can, and if you can't I'll take an I.O.U. Good champagne, bad champagne, mediocre champagne. It's all good. Beneath the makeup of the mask of the fabricated character on the illusory dais in the false premise of the empty dialogue deep within the preposterous life, lies life. Alone in our little room we watch the shadows concoct the facts between us. One day they'll learn to speak but what ears will we have to listen, what words to reply? Meet my integrity, he wags his tail so dutifully whereas yours bares its teeth, so pure, so true. Oil. Balm. Unguent. Ambrosia. Vapour. Sleep. One day, long ago, I lost my sock in the laundromat of laugh. The pineal gland throbs in the ganglion of the blind fish in the dark of the Mariana Trench, while in me and in the ancient me it has no apparent purpose other than to squirm at fluorescent light, housing the tiny pebble I once called myself. Boil that soup of ashes and rain, paste my gills shut. Let me rewrite that silence. You'll thank me for it later. On the two headlands, two fires signaling in foreign codes. The wood they burn is different. Their smoke unlike our smoke. The silhouettes of my ancestors dancing before the sparks I do not recognize. My father did not ask to be born. Yet here we are. The angel of irritability stretches her elbows on the head of this overcrowded pin. A triumvirate of avenues all ending in the same place: You. Me. We. In the closet of my body a basketful of search warrants. The wafer of moon in my mouth, dissolution's loveliness. The endless criterion of sitting very still. Idle. Idyll. Informality suits my temperament. What, sir, suits yours? From your aura I bet I can guess your school. In my wardrobe a metaphor. Wear it well. I do. In the theatre of cardboard one word brings us inevitably to the next. At the edge of the abyss autumn takes its cue. Jump, fugitive, escape the fear of fear. Beneath the layers of my awfulness a tiny incorruptible, my residue after all the other agencies have taken their cut. Welcome to the church of bewilderment where faith never wavers. In your dreams the answer to everything, in my dreams the question. In the steaks frying on the griddle, in the crackle of salt in the wave's song, hear the static of applause.

Midnight again. Time for work. Unstitch that wound. Let the wolf lick your wrist. Awaiting the disease, the kettle hisses its quiet panacea. It's formulaic but we get there. The rules of chance are a straitjacket. Don't forget to breathe. In the stone's pith an echo of the flint. All that is held in my hand is lost from my hand, but the memory of your hand reaching out. What price this lovely afternoon? Nothing. It's free. Remember? The stone waits for the glacier to wake it, nudge it along to its fulfillment: a nicer view, or a worse. Your breath circulates its own vapour where all is one, and all is two, and all is whole.

Charles D'Anastasi

Lodgers

You have only to consider the determination with which they single out the world for close dissection, the way they lacerate in the early morning light, the way they pirouette with glee, once convinced their words have found the right spot. As if their raison d'etre depends on their own life hanging in the balance—scavengers, feeding on the breadcrumbs of discarded thoughts and words. It's obvious that something in them is easily swayed by the sky's hard blue, the slenderness of some-one's wrist, or the almost-not-there torso in the dark. There's no point in wondering at the desire with which they rally round the moon, clusters of spinifex in red desert sand, or the hem of a fine mist at the foot of Uluru. Or the way they're convinced that theirs' is the one song that will make you break down and weep, as they keep on insisting on shaping or unshaping the hours, trying to improve that which they cannot explain. Then there's the ease with which they step in and out of mirrors for their own or the public's delectation, or the way they make a virtue of sliding through newly found, dimly lit, neoned laneways, in one of those damaged cities of the night. And there's not much to be done, if you wake up one day with a vague, nagging feeling of unease, only to find one or more of them had taken up rooms in the furthest corner of your mind -lodgers who are only too pleased to remind you that they have their work to do—and besides, they had already paid up a few years' rent in advance.   28

Trina Denner

Playing Outside

Fluorescent shoes sprint past. The soles, chunked with blue and green rubber innovations, wave at us.

'He must be doing a tempo run,' Paul says, our feet hitting the pavement in tandem.

'Yeah.'

I watch the guy pass. Orbs of sweat leap off his body in explosive arcs.

Without consultation, we speed up.

'You got netball this morning?' I ask.

'Yep,' he draws breath. 'Simone's team's playing the Amazonians.'

'Nice name.'

He snorts. 'They might be twelve, but I wouldn't back myself in an arm wrestle with a couple of 'em.'

I take my eyes off where my feet are landing to look sideways. 'It's the hormones in chicken.'

He smiles.

'You?' he questions.

'Nah, they've done nothing for me.'

He laughs.

'I'm on the soccer run,' I say. 'Gotta have two kids on different fields at the same time.'

I jump sideways onto the grass to avoid a lady leading a Schnauzer. Its tail is erect: the sceptre of The Path Monarch. I get a whiff of lavender talc, but it's gone, and the earthiness of the brook is back in my nostrils.

A string of bikes approach from the other direction.

Paul leaps off the other side, 'Shit.' His shoe sinks into the mud that skulks beneath the grass.

We reunite beyond the interruptions, moving south-poled magnets pointed towards a common north.

'Bloody cyclists.' He mutters. 'Why don't they keep their lycra-clad arses off the bike paths, and on the road where they belong?'

I smile. Last week they needed to stay off the roads.

'Grown men do not wear pink,' he adds.

'And the women?'

He grunts.

'You're a colour bigot. Boys can wear pink.'

'But they shouldn't.'

'Homophobe,' I tease.

'Girl,' he throws back.

We run. I feel prickling on my skin where the sweat congregates at the small of my back. I reach behind and unstick the fabric of my shirt. It flops immediately back. I can smell the must of my sports bra; $19.95 worth of absorptive memory, of sweat and kilometres run in the Queensland sun.

'Are you coming to Club this week?'

'Nah.' His head is shaking in my peripheral vision. 'The wife's taken up yoga.'

'What? On a Tuesday night?'

He sounds miffed. 'We're taking turns, week about. Apparently we live in a democracy.'

I chuckle, despite my annoyance. 'Can't she pick another night?'

'I've told her that old birds don't do yoga. They'll break a hip.'

'How'd that go down?'

'Whatdya reckon? She took me apart.'

I knew Pam. I knew that was a lie.

'She said the class was full of all sorts, and I should come along—' his words were punctuated with panted hyphens '— might help my running.'

I smirk. 'Sounds appealing.'

'I'll tell you next week.'

'You're going?' I slow up, letting him move through the footbridge before me. I watch his shoulder blades swing beneath his singlet; his wiry arms relaxed as Sunday brunch.

'I can't imagine there's much stretch in those spindly legs, Paul.'

'The bloody insolence,' he says in mock-horror.

I know he likes the jibes. Gives us something to talk about.

'But compared to the Gen-Ys, I'm incredibly well behaved,' I announce. My mind wanders to the grey hairs I've been finding at my temples, plucking them out by the roots.

He harrumphs.

I speed up to get back alongside as we cruise into the street where Paul lives. The last stretch is uphill. We push; I see my car parked a way off. I imagine my water bottle, warm from sitting in the sun on the passenger seat. I can taste it running down my throat.

I jump a broken bottle, its label holds together some of the glass carnage. I land with a crunch at the edge of the splatter pattern.

We stop at the mailbox. Number 23. Michael Jordan's number. It's an unspoken finishing marker. To stop before would

31

be certain failure. Once reached, we're free to palaver around the driveway like drunken pigeons, hands—wings—on hips.

'How far'd we go?'

Paul brings his GPS watch up close to his eyes and fiddles with the buttons.

'Twenty three point four,' he says. 'Good pace, too. We were doing 4'45"s most of the way.'

I nod. It was a solid run.

We sit down on the steps. I loosen my laces, pulling one shoe off with two hands, inspecting the tread for hints of glass.

Paul stands. 'Wanna beer?'

I screw up my face, looking into the sun as he stands before me. 'It's morning.'

'And it's bloody hot. We've earned it.'

He wanders off inside and I hear the fridge door open with a resistant schmock.

Yeah, I guess we have.

Richard Holt

The Swimmer

One morning, while running, Ollie Perovic thought he spotted a swimmer momentarily within the featurelessness of the new day's grey, but he couldn't be sure. There was no colour, no contrast. No light or dark. No horizon. Later he imagined perhaps he heard a distant voice calling but, as it was early spring, plenty of boisterous groups were using the foreshore—boot camp warriors and football clubs—so he thought nothing of it. No one passed as he trudged up the hill to the beacon and over to the footbridge.

Only later that day, as he headed back to the office from Soup King, did Ollie recall the two possibilities, the swimmer and the voice, each as uncertain as each other. The coincidence of these memories brought about a kind of dread, which stuck with him all afternoon. He was unable to concentrate on the Pathways Report and found himself checking online news sites every few minutes. Though the media reported no one missing, his brooding uncertainty persisted.

A week later, as he shuffled along the sand of Eastern Beach in the thickness of another fog he heard a call from the direction of the waves. He pulled off his running shoes and t-shirt and leapt into the water. He was a better swimmer than runner and had put three hundred metres between himself and the shore before he realised the icy conditions were getting the better of him. His limbs began to cramp. An all-over shiver ran through him. Looking to the shore he could just make out a figure on the beachside path, jogging in a heavy, plodding gait that seemed familiar. Ollie Perovic called, across the waves with all that was left of his flagging strength.

Monica Goldberg

The line with arms

'*The moment of change is the only poem*—Adrienne Rich

Still. We Wait. For the strangers that are hiding. Fractured ones, that are not. Yet visible to the naked eye. The tension that proves. That the world is not rigid. Only searching—for its equilibrium, point. The hoist that can not. Stay where it is and will not move. Either. That wobbles around its axis. That knows how to push.

Boundaries.

That will not travel— in perfect lines. That depart from their cultural path. That will not spin out or settle. Into stable rotation and refuse to ignore. The interaction of opposing forces. The random— and the systematic. The imperceptible and inevitable. The evolution of language. The meaning that is abandoned. The moment of change.

Jessica McLean

Nearby

We're going camping on the Keep River, a one and a half hour drive from Kununurra. The dirt road crosses two creeks to get to the best camping spots on the river; it's worth it. The Keep invites wallabies and kangaroos down, thousands of birds including jabirus, brolgas and magpie geese. Some people, like my two camping friends, go there to try and catch fish like the elusive Barramundi. I don't fish though. I prefer to watch the river and the animals using it. And then, when the sun disappears, I watch the stars above and the fire at our feet—an outdoor television—and we talk about falling in love and sex and eat killer chocolate cake and drink a full bottle of whiskey to empty.

I leave that conversation without knowing it, too tired for many good reasons, one of them being immersed in a close and raw nature. It is enervating being in country that you have to be very careful in, for the Keep houses crocodiles and unlike the Ord, its neighbour, dams do not prevent their upstream migration. All night long the sensation of having an animal about to pull me down to the muddy banks and under the water for a death roll seeps in and out of my consciousness. Somewhere before dawn my feet start to feel like blocks of ice.

I wake in the pre-dawn darkness and huddle closer to the fire. A fire that is not alight anymore. The first (irrational?) thought I have is *I wonder if there's a saltie in our camp?* I reason that, even if she were wandering around our riverside camp, the green coloured swag might camouflage me. She would not be able to see me, my ignorant wasted brain asserted. I lie still then, with shallow breath, keeping the canvas over my head just as it had enclosed me all night, for what I could not see could not hurt.

The birds start flying overhead with the slight breaking of light. It sounds like a big flock of ducks. Don't know what sort because I refuse to look out from my cocoon until the sun is higher in the sky. As night falls away, I assume that the crocodile, if it is nearby, would also go. I don't want to risk eye contact with a saltie from my extremely compromised position.

With the coming of full sun, I peel the canvas back off my head to see one of my co-campers walking the twenty metres to the river edge. She quietly tells me that there is a croc swimming in the water. I go down to the river and there it floats—its body submerged but looking up and out, towards us, from a few metres upstream. We pack up our gear and load the four wheel drive.

As we are about to leave, A Miriwoong man and his kids come by our camp site, they pause for a moment to assess our camping spot before we head back to town.

Looks good here. You know Blackie? This is his spot, just downstream here. He's 24 foot long. His missus lives over there. He's probably been watching you mob all the time you know.

Later that day, we drive by our spot after taking a reconnaissance mission further north towards the river's mouth, and there on the opposite bank, twenty metres or so apart, lie two salties, one much bigger than the other. Blackie and his missus, we figure.

Sylvia Petter

Bat-apple Pie

Here, where we live, out in the sticks, we've got fruit trees galore
—apples, mostly—and the bats love 'em! Not your cricket bats,
mind, although the kids do run about swinging one at the other,
trying to whack them.

I'm torn, you see. Those little creatures—nothing like Dracula
at all. My favourite's the broad-nosed bat with his black nose and
bits of pink fur. I'd just love them to keep away from the apples,
and I'd love the kids to leave the bats alone. I mean, they do
eat up all the mozzies, and I bet if they had a place to hang out
together where a gang of kids couldn't bash them, well, we'd all
get on. And I could give 'em a trough of fallen apples as a reward.
Make everyone happy. And the kids could get back to playing
cricket with those bits of wood they found.

Saw a postcard once about bats hanging up, like out on the
line, like out to dry. I think it was some sort of sculpture. But a
great idea. Trouble is, the Hills Hoist got stunned by lightning a
few months ago. Well, it wasn't a real one, they're too expensive
for round here, but it was close. Now what if I got it back together
again and put it down the back, away from the apples. I could
thread old mouldy apples on to the wires. Dress it up a bit. It'd
look like Christmas. The bats could hang there and nibble, too
high for the kids to reach.

Just a thought. If they all came we might have to cull them.
Wonder if you can eat them. Times are tough, but they tell me
they breed quick. Bat-apple pie?

Hilary Hewitt

saturday barbie

the carpenter is a hunk/ out of stock @ alexandria/ cowgirl boots
on heading west to ashfield with erwn i don't tweet & drive/ pira-
nhamatta road sez erwn sometimes i laugh at his jokes/ 2 many
car yards good taste is simple black porsche vintage merc prius all
good/ rusted iron console à la country trader @ junkyard under
railway bridge/ lycra in bus lane/ need clover as premier/ grrl
power/ i care about environment 2/ climate change happening
4 real out here erwn says porsche v fuel-efficient switch on a-c/
liquor barn detour moët my fave 3 4 2 i fill the boot erwn flashes
his plastic/ kiss kiss

queue like topshop at turn 2 bunningstown/ sizzle in carpark/ not
talking chorizos/ who knew erwn fancies barbq sangas?/ tomato
sauce stains/ numbered aisles bigger than ikea industrial chic/ a
greeter in pre-xmas gear (red green etc) not sure about apron/
the elf likes my shirt—hot pink on trend—sez his ex b/friend in
fashion 2/ erwn still at sossie stand/ does pork help sperm count?/
elfie gives me a tour older men in leafblowers couples in gardening
buying their widgers and dibbers those cheeky chinese/ i'm an
early adopter / sure will be if erwn keeps shooting blanks/ 2 many
hot doggies

spot lime green twirly clothes line/ neons so now in milan/ i hang
up my shirt quite a crowd not like i'm topless (try tamarama)/ my

new citrus bra/ lemon pegs work well with clothes lines/ we sell out of both my top goes as well tell elfie to order aqua tango and musk/ tea break/ erwn asleep in front seat/ load moëts in trolley someone pinches my butt is there an aisle-high club best party in years/ elfie has headache/ make him nest in cream hessian (shadecloth 2 scratchy) put on green apron tell crowd i'm filling in/ someone laughs/ say what you like about saline i'll never regret getting these breast implants

aisle 32 closed/ conga line 2 bath-wear my tap tour at 12 how to avoid droopy spouts/ man in black beckons oh oh/ hardware arms/ might be a bouncer/ chasings past nuts and bolts he's panting 2 better than sexpo let him catch me in tools/ feeling quite hot must have ovul8'd/ OMG marco's in marketing wants 2 talk figures photoshoots he likes my bra i like his moves/ aisle 10 closed/ empties in green bin/ erwn taking elf home/ recycling good 4 environment/ clover 4 premier/ marco 4 me/ we're going 2 practise our salsa/ m rides a black norton knows hot retro motel/ head'n down the h'way/ to the el dorado/ purple rain/ emu plains

jenni nixon

bear that is not

a koala is asleep in the eucalypt tree-fork high above my
squinting self in the sunset darkening outside our ensuite cabin
by the myall shores where waders stand all leggy at the water's
edge and the ferryman waits for coin. fossils found of some kind
of koala date back twenty-five million years a bear that is not a
bear *phascolarctos cinereus* meaning *ash grey pouched bear* thought
to be like a teddy bear is *an arboreal herbivorous marsupial native
to australia and only extant representative of the family phasco-
larctidae.* breeding only once a year a female has blind hairless
baby joeys that crawl into her pouch when about an inch long.
koala bear facts say they need a lot of space for their societies and
after one has died other koalas *usually won't move into the vacant
territory for about a year or until scent markings and scratches of
the old owner disappear.* aboriginal names include *koalas koolas
karbors koolewongs* and may mean *no drink.* according to an
aboriginal myth if the body of a dead koala is not treated with
respect the spirit of *koorbo* causes rivers to dry and people to die
of thirst. the koala stares down at me before shifting weight to
fall back to sleep while in the bluegreen sea over the sand-dunes
pods of dolphins in wetsuits surf the waves as a whale further out
is breaching its tail smacking the sea. on the dirt road to pacific
palms a dingo is running bloodied from a large rock thrown by
campers. as a kid with my family we passed myall lakes then

crossed to tuncurry from forster by car-ferry when travelling up
north at christmastime. we did not stop for scenery or to look at
birds wombats or kangaroos. i heard barking. is she protecting
territorial rights or mourning their destruction? hazy memories
of bush fire devastation chance survival when hunted as food
and fur or to escape the fangs of wild dogs snarling? the road-kill
screech of braking vehicles burning tyres that disturbs her sleep?
is she hallucinating the unstoppable deliberately introduced cane
toads jumping across kakadu that keep breeding with no natural
predators a major threat to native animals or lamenting bees
wiped out from pesticides or something else? worker-bees staging
a spring offensive lost revolutionary uprising against the queen
turning the sky black? or is a nightmare of the dead and dying
white carcass of the barrier reef smothered in toxic dredge spoil
with all the pretty fishies vanished in the too warm rising of
the sea scary enough for her to scuttle away to some ethereal
safety? in ten years numbers are down by ninety percent owing to
disease—chlamydia can cause blindness and pneumonia—or the
foxes or feral cats that prey upon the young. koala habitat logged
for roads to mcmansions sixbedrooms fivebathrooms and more
roads for grazing cattle timber trucks and hunters with rifles in
national parks. open-cut coal mines in forests the fracking coal
seam gas leaking methane polluted water ecological disasters or
entire picturesque valleys covered by coal and petroleum explo-
ration. without a plan our natural world tree-snuggled koalas
all the beauty's feathered whirr iridescence wild bird calling is
silenced and forever departed.

Stu Hatton

down south

Mangrove salts. Beachside bins reek of prawn-shell traces. Resorts polish ecstasy down to a fine star. Pour a flagship red, then another. Kids're bred tough here, bob through churns of surf...while cocky, ageing rubbernecks get dumped, spat, graze-limbed. Beachgoers step through gazes; some sunbaker perves through chinks in the straw hat that roofs his face from the noon. Chopper hovers, spreads concentrics over ocean, sounds the shark alarm. Up the bluff there's a cave of bone, which might be called the skull. For 'those who forget to leave', read 'those who turn to sand'.

Yallingup, WA.

Jeremy Page

the brown country

vegemite toast for breakfast. skip lunch. draped in a towel still damp with yesterday we drift over the dunes, our calloused feet sinking deep in the hot sand. this is what we starved ourselves for.

stretched on the sand we soak in sunlight. drenched with the sea we wade in, wade out. swallow salt. the sun slides down the horizon as our pink skin still pulses with latent heat. it might storm. bundle wet towels into the boot. hot seatbelts, cold air whips through the window. lime and coronas in an eski for dinner. a few cigarettes. drawing deep on the nicotine we line our lungs thick with black tar. light brown freckles scatter along our shoulders like vegemite stains. day in, day out. all summer, until we die. and our bronzed and red freckled bodies are buried beneath the brown earth, our flesh sinking into the soil, becoming salty food for the small brown earthworms.

Paul Mitchell

The Old Man and the Pool

What's it like to be old, I asked the old man in the pool, his grey hair wetted back at the sides and he smiled at me like he'd been waiting to hear that question for his entire life or more. How old are you? he asked me. I'm thirty-one just gone, I told him, and I swished the water in front of me quickly. A kid dived in and splashed us, the water was cold on my back and I shivered and lowered myself to keep as warm as I could. What's it like being thirty-one? he asked and I told him it was better than thirty, thirty's a fat number, but thirty-one feels skinny, like a kid just getting started riding on training wheels, getting some balance. The old man ran his hand through his hair like someone might be tricked into thinking he was good looking. That's what being old is like, he said, like your bicycle's skinny and you can't get your balance because the pool has an eye on you and you'll never dive into your body or splash a question again. Then he swam away with quick kicks that didn't get him anywhere fast, just left me cold enough to shiver against the rail.

Anna Kerdijk Nicholson

At Sculpture by the Sea

Turning a corner, a man in well-cut casual clothes is snarling
over a boy whose arms he has crossed over the child's chest so
the child's shoulder blades wing and whose wrists he now pulls
apart so the sockets look like they'll pop and if this is what he
does in public how much more elsewhere, the muscle on his arm
the size of the child's skull.

My *What the hell do you think you're doing* washes up on the
rocks near the resin echidnas and the kid's eyes shut, his thin
legs buckle and the crowd moves on and round.

Pawel Cholewa

'There's a Road Train Going Nowhere'

We begin to drive westward, departing from Townsville and into the night. A sense of energy, excitement and apprehension circulates within and around us. We grow silent, but why? Is it difficult to leave the comfort of the coast, perhaps? The coast makes sense. It had always made sense. It was difficult letting go of that logic. Trees thinned and ranges flattened into the isolated plains and scrublands that grew more and more unfamiliar in their destitute simplicity. The echoes from the crashing surf and bustling city centre and the general roar of the population subsided and penetrated no longer. Our silence turns into contemplation, turns into meditation, turns into a respectable isolation and still we continue to drive, breaking free from the edges of the world as we drive further away from its fringes.

Music is playing. In fact, it had always been playing in the car, but we only just realised that. We are waiting for something; something big, ominous, threatening. We'd all heard stories about road trains leading up to this journey, but none of us had ever seen one, and nobody wanted to be the one who had to tackle a road train from within the insignificance and (dis) comfort of our automobile. The music grows louder, or seems louder. A throbbing and cyclical bass line, and in the midst of a wailing, dissonant harmonica growls the vocal sensibilities of a young, impassioned Peter Garrett, proclaiming and announcing, 'There's a road train going nowhere.' And coincidentally, right at that moment, the road train manifests. The great mammoth of Australian pride and industry, transportation and solidity. A beast foreboding, forbearing and ingraining itself into the earth around us, trembling, shaking, determined it growls rising from the horizon before us. Lights. Its dark shape creeps forward as we hurry or scuttle to catch up to it. It is a giant, a titan of production and productivity. Rogue and nomadic in essence, it knowingly owns and rides that road.

A monochromatic sheen coats its body, its armour. Too many wheels and too many metres long. Signposted in black and yellow, a fair warning is given to the oblivious, to the naïve and to the overly ambitious. An anonymous driver resides within never to be seen by others on the road, except for perhaps by other drivers of other road trains and the 'other' in more generalised or metaphysical ways. They control the habitat of these barren roads. We must be respectful to them or perish.

Shrubbery flies in front and behind us. A kangaroo leaps. Cicadas fizzle and chime. But the ratios of the animalistic and natural world are all skewed and wrong in comparison to this unifying unit. So grand, so large, so overwhelmingly powerful it dominates the night sky creating a black hole of some sort unto itself. All the powers of the world seep into it. The night turns light by comparison. I think I can still see the Sun gleaming somewhere off in the distance but I can't exactly pinpoint it—the road train is silhouetted by the powers of the world.

But where is the road train going? Is Garrett correct? Is it going nowhere? It's certainly not stuck or stationary. It has motion and momentum and speed, yet it continues to drive into nothingness, into the outback of absurdity and delirium, into nowhere. It goes because it needs to go. It propels and projects itself. Its purpose is grander than what we are led to believe. Its journey and travels are both the means and the ends of its existence. Through universe and time and change it persists and endures as a perpetual icon of Australian industry and power.

Across the great red plains of the Australian outback the road spirals into the centre of an old prehistoric world, dried up. The road train conquers, controls, manoeuvres this road. They were built to be here and exist here together. A peaceful harmony, an omnipresent synchronisation, unified by the smoky black tyres that the road train attaches itself to the road with, gliding, soaring into the tranquil inverse universe that is the National Highway.

Very close now. We are right behind it. It shudders. No, we shudder at the prospect of having to somehow actually 'pass' this titan. No, no one will do it. Respect the giant. Leave it be. It owns the road. It owns the night. It owns itself. We will not overtake the road train this night.

Anna Kerdijk Nicholson

The mind travels

A stream of brown trout in a shallow river, the mind travels so much faster than language, that laggard which if you try to get it by the scruff eludes while the brain's already gone through Harold Pinter's *The Caretaker* and an image of the characters on stage, compared it to a Manchester production of *Godot* seen in the round and how the rails at one's feet bit into one's arches, the sparse leaves on the tree at the end (ah there is hope), the journey to *Caretaker* in York down the A59 driving in Mum's maroon mini, D shouting at the other drivers 'what the fuck, can't you drive, can't you see we need to be let in' and a couple of near head-ons, to sit there in the dark to be coruscated and all that in the time it took to write the words after 'laggard' and before 'eludes', how can we capture the trout which have moved darkly, playing three dimensional chess with their speckled glistening bodies, beauty unheralded, unsung.

Jude Aquilina

Bus Drivers

Mean ones skid on puddles beside busy bus-stops; slam doors in faces; ignore voices and knockings; pull away from breathless old ladies with shopping bags and begging eyes. These domino-loving drivers lean on brakes or accelerate before we reach our seats, topple children over, dislocate the shoulders of straphangers. The nice drivers pull over before or after stops; say, 'Good morning'; help mothers with pushers; let schoolkids on who've lost their tickets. These drivers often whistle or sing—they are the great modern people herders, guiding their flocks through perilous traffic. And what if, on this hot January afternoon, at peak hour, our smiling driver locks pneumatic doors and ferries us off official routes to the beach. Imagine the faces he'd see in his mirror; I know that thick air of silence as passengers stare at each other when a bus takes a wrong turn. Now picture us as the bus hits wet sand and we're told no one's going home till they've swam, eaten hot chips (at State Transport's expense) and fed the seagulls. Thank you, handsome driver, humming a Beach Boys tune, for giving this sheep's imagination room to roam and for guiding me safely home through traffic jams and fantasies.

Moya Costello

Arts and Crafts at the Agricultural Show

'You can't top a Turnstile Moment,' is what you think as you enter the Show Grounds.

'You pay your coins to the ferryman ...'

A rough passage in the borderland is not out of the question. But you keep journeying in transition: the turnstile swings you forward—and you're there, you've crossed over to the other side.

Inside the grounds, you're undecided what to do first, where to go, decide to check the map, while familiar imagery fills your senses from this new world that is the showgrounds. The Ferris wheel circles with its complement of blind faith. Fairy floss gathers on a stick in its wonder-making machine, a nest of electrified hair becoming a ball of air in the mouth, synthesising to a sticky grit of small pink jewels. The rainbow-coloured blades of hand-held wind twirls recall liquidity and tall windmills in the stark aridity of Australia's outback. Slouch hats for the sun are suddenly commonplace, as if the showgrounds themselves were the site of a specific breeding and housing program. And the kewpie dolls remind you of Ladies Lounges.

Far from the Ladies Lounges, in the Arts and Crafts pavilion, Florence, Jessie, Maude, Eily, Lily and Dolly made the jams and pickles and passionfruit butter. Are the jars of bottled fruit to be opened and their contents eaten? The display of perfection is disconcerting when you don't stack obsessively to a Geometric Rule of Law yourself. The bottles are exquisitely, excruciatingly, exactingly packed, the geometry at odds with the luminosity and warmth of the bottles infused with comfort. The jars could be opened onto a rush of colour for the eyes and perfume for the nose, against the depths of winter's cold and dark, in an eating of summer on the lips and tongue.

Might you cut into the thickness of almond paste, bite into a sugar leaf, and discover, underneath, flour, fruit and egg? The fruit cake halves, placed at angles, one half over the other, look like the dismantled blocks from wood chopped in the arena, ready for devouring by saliva, by flame.

Where did they—the cooks, preservers, decorators, knitters, embroiderers—get such nerve, such persistence, confidence, energy, time? You can't imagine doing these things for competition.

The judges look in the half-sliced fruit cake for fruit and peel evenly cut and distributed, an absence of damp spots, no 'tunnels', no crust. They complain in their Judges' Report that contestants aren't bothered to read the competition schedule where those seated in judgement had scrupulously laid out the rules for creative engagement. An iced cake meant iced on top only, and several contestants went blithely ahead and iced the whole—top and sides. And went mad with orange peel in their orange cakes, embedding it on the icing, as well as in the cake. In the damper section, they baked in a tin. Such entries displayed undisciplined practice, anarchically inclined behaviour, and were eliminated from the competition. Scones, said the Judges' Report, were often doughy, large and tough, covered in flour, baked in contact with each other, when a scone was supposed to be light as air, nicely coloured, free of flour bathing, delicate and discreet, fully rounded and definitely not showing in their sculptural form the intrusive weight of other scones.

Your mother's scones were small and imperfect, rocky as a barren landscape. But you've never eaten one that you've enjoyed as much as hers.

You think of the status of your own knitted patchwork blanket: the antithesis of perfection, the apotheosis of roughness. Mismatched scraps of wool, angora and cotton, in different ply knitted with differently sized needles. No tension. Colour match awry. Sizing of patches deregulated. Dropped stitches. Idiosyncratic experimental combinations of purl and plain. Squares so roughly knitted, they unravelled on completion. The stitching attaching one patch to the other undone before the blanket was in use. Stitches lost in spaces; spaces made by lost stitches making holes as you drag it out by a corner on a cold night, to wrap it round yourself and another patch stretched in this rough usage comes asunder from its companion to whom its temporary, rail attachment is visible in a large gap barred with loosening sinews. But this blanket is a blanket, surprisingly warm. It does its job. The point, for you, is never to create a perfect imitation.

Moving on to the needlework, you remember that you love a good doily, full of holes as they are. In the long display lines, you recognise the mania for making copies, learning by imitation. *The Blue Boy* and the ancient Egyptians, Nefertiti and Tutankhamen, are common sources of work for the tapestry makers. But *sic faciunt omnes*: everyone does it. Think minor character in Verrocchio's *The Baptism of Christ*, angel on the left—and you'll get the picture.

Barrie Walsh

Howbeit I Howszat

Howbeit I haven't proof typifies Spring Racing Carnival 2012 Victoria Derby Day's Salinger, also called Yellowglen Stakes Saturday 3 November controversy, at least as quantitative measure, 0-to-8 digit Magic 3-Square 12-sacred insight.

7	2	3
0	4	8
5	6	1

Magic 3 square
12 secret number

Stewards question *Howmuchdoyouloveme* to Group-2 race favourite after 'racing investigation unit found Hessian bag full of instruments used to stomach drench a horse. Trainer Con Karakatsanis' father Tony argued he simply picked-up the wrong bag, believing it contained a biscuit of hay. With investigations on-going, *Howmuchdoyouloveme* raced but wasn't placed.'

Codename Sherbet's reference:

KJV Ruth 3.12: And now it is true that I am thy near kinsman: howbeit there is a kinsman nearer than I.

as 1-to-9 digits Magic 3-Square's secret number's 15 & 1611 King James Bible's 1ˢᵗ Edition Ruth 3.15 'He/She went in to the city' 2-printrun error.

Howbeit's peculiar to KJV Ruth 3.12, & 12th-word from the beginning is end-paired with am *1ˢᵗperson singular present tense of be, &/or ante-meridiem abbreviation Latin=before noon.*

As Derby Day's 'race that stops the nation' foreplay, Sherbet entered the equation's *3-dot-pyramid* math symbol 'therefore', not pulling up stumps as Saturday to Tuesday's 3-days is 4-sacred hides plain-sight, for cricketers' question needs asking, as unless they walk, you can't get batsmen out.

'It's why the 12th-man's gagged; can't get your own team out.'

Sherbet's making contact. Plenty of time to appeal_

'Leg-square's right-angle,' he agrees with another: $5^2=3^2+4^2$ & $5+3+4=12$.

'Great song,' he replies. Suddenly the wicket's sticky. Some find sickly, others slippery. It's as different as salt & sugar; inorganic & organic science calls vitalism, but Sherbet knows it's bitter-sweet. 'Playwright Kit Marlowe's codenamed Sweet as Walsingham spy to Elizabethan theatre's hive of prime meridian espionage, as nation solving *Contact-Zero* ruled 'where am I' seas.

4	9	2
3	5	7
8	1	6

Magic 3 square
15 secret number

4	9	2
3	1	7
8	5	6

Purifying Fire
1/5 Interchange

4	9	2
C	1	7
H	E	6

Chloe
Speedie Code

Intro ghostwriter Chloe Speedie, as Sherbet probes:

'Organic burns; inorganic doesn't, differentiating life & non-life, give or take the dead. Transmutation explains secret 15, but what's 12-entity?'

Asked to explain, Sherbet deflects.

'Infinitely many infinite universes, ask Chloe.'

Sherbet wipes sweat. Is it fear?

Ghostwriter focuses on MOVE 3rd-&-4th letters VE=225=15^2=9^2+12^2 codes OIL is today's *Contact-Zero* endgame.

Sherbet pads-up; uncertain if he's next in or silly-mid-wicket.

$15+9+12=36=6^2$: so 18-character *Howmuchdoyouloveme* only half the story. Dropping 'How' is secret-15, whereas 12 appeals 'Howyou'.

Punters on edge: Chloe juxtaposes MOVE/LOVE storytelling's MEL is $13^2=5^2+12^2$ Federation Square fractal façade; isn't sacred architecture awesome, Sherbet's at Winterthur HIH interface to Australia's largest corporate collapse, $5.3-billion estimated lost March 15, 2001 liquidation, the vault's last-guard defense encrypted, post-function.

Chancing 1st-person 'I' is Roman numeral 1, its opening reveals Winterthur HIH initial coding WHoneH reversed reads Hone HW=823.

The STIFF Code's YNOT intel's correct. There's no 'honey', Jerusalem's 669-listings in The Bible's Old Testament & 154 in the New, total 823.

Corporate Australia knows Winterthur sold its 51% share 1999 after taking company public 4 years earlier, so when Australia's 2nd largest Insurance collapsed within 2 years of Winterthur's exit, to Australians caught, its HIH. Fraudulent on multiple fronts, including 'I' is one, Sherbet realizes it's a tomb; misleading trails to certain death without decryption.

Win-t-erthur juxtaposed Win-t-Arthur highlights AE=15 sacred to Knights Round Table while Winterthur as Winter-&-thur-shuffle=Ruth. Sherbet selected HI-tripled as 81818/777=1053; *Contact-Zero*'s number of fishes to The Bible's 153 feeding people, & reversed IH-tripled 181818/777=234 St Georges Day as Shakespeare's d-o-b; d-o-d.

Shock, horror, *Howmuchdoyouloveme* controversy coincides public announcement Princess Shert Nebti tomb discovery, Egypt, proves Sherbet's investigations compromised. Leaving vault to warn Chloe, HoneH to Arcadia codes NR interchange & H=S atbash-sequence fixates HORSE, underestimates maze Deconstruction lost cause 400th Regiomontanus 'doomsday-prophecy' Comet 1588 to différance: *origin of presence & absence, the hinge between outer meaning & inner representation.*

Trace Uncanny A*topia Fiction 1988: bee-motif is part of many cultures. Egyptians considered bees sacred, bridging natural & underworlds.

Sherbet grasps sacred future; Hexagon Star of David, Solomon Seal's dice-5 tipping Melbourne Cup 2012 winner overrides Headquarters Tavern Plate Race-10 illegal stomach-pump #5 *Beseech* anagrams *bee-sec-H.*

Problem is Winterthur HIH lockdown, therefore ghostwriter Chloe needs perception, *arche*-writing text=context getting story out, some contained within i.e. Shakespeare based *A Winter's Tale* on Robert Greene's 1588 novel *Pandosto: The Triumph of Time.* 1st person to record in death-bed coded-writing, meeting Shakespeare, novel's reprinted *Dorastus & Fawnia* 1607 Virginia Company's America settlement, Jamestown, aligns Halley's Comet.

Ghostwriter différance: rogue ex-CIA Hand formed Nugan Hand Bank financed Asia heroine-trafficking using Nugan's 1970's Australian marijuana-route, supplanting A-NZ-US cannabis. After bank's collapse, Hand disappeared using Alan Winter false-passport, one of planet's most wanted.

Invisible worlds exist in architecture, as HIH codifies.

Chloe's incommunicado with Sherbet, so uses Howszat contingency black-&-white Derby Day, pronounced Darby, AE=15 encodes Magic 3-Square, All Black AB=12 other.

On the wallaby's a transient swag searching work.

Wallaby of a question's finding an Aussie Melbourne Cup stayer.

Is getting into post-GFC black's dark-world before the next collapse a matter of getting Sherbet out?

Lynette Washington

The Swarm

The others have gone to sleep. I sit with him on the balcony smoking weed that I acquired for this purpose - the reward after the climb. We blow blue-grey smoke into the air and pass the small joint between us, careful to avoid touching, though I place the damp roll of paper to my lips with delicate desire.

A forest of Casuarina trees stands in front of us and the blazing moon tips over the apex of the highest tree. The view from our cabin is not expansive; it's homely in its closed-in smallness.

I ache to tell him but it will jeopardise two precious things. We talk about the inconsequential and I lazily drift off into imagined worlds where it would be OK for me to admit my secret. These places are thrilling and dangerous. I want to be dangerous instead of protecting my precarious and imperfect life.

The joint is gone and I am joyous and hungry and pleasantly lightheaded. Now is the time, if there would ever be a time. I can use the drug as an excuse so that we can pretend I never actually said something from which there is no return.

I stand and prepare to go inside, straightening my bulky jacket and wriggling my numb toes in their stiff, muddy boots. I stamp the mud off.

Well, we did it, I say. The summit. I keep my tone level.

He stands too. We don't hug as a rule, but the joint has freed us of this particular inhibition and we take a step towards each other with our arms half raised, eliminating the careful space I have kept all throughout the hike. This is my opportunity for the contact I crave. I will make the most of it. I lean my body into him so that we connect from our thighs through our hips and to our cheeks. I take a breath, slowly in, feeling his body move with mine, and slowly out. I hold him longer than would be considered appropriate, but he holds me too.

He turns his head and I feel his breath flow over the exposed skin of my neck carrying a soft humidity that hints of the tropics in this cold forest and spreading goose bumps down my shoulders. My skin puckers and bursts through the warmth of my thermals. This air expelled from deep within him arouses me beyond reason.

We do not let go.

I smell the sweetness of the joint in his hair and feel the thickness of his arms around me and catalogue them, file them into my memory. I will need them later when I am scolding myself for both holding him too long, and for not telling him this one thing.

The time to end this indulgent moment has passed.

His lips press into the nape of my neck. He is hesitant, as though he's giving himself the option of calling it an accident. But my intake of breath is so sharp and desirous that he cannot mistake my response. He continues. My eyes are closed against the forest and my thighs lean further into his, this time for support rather than clandestine touch. His kiss explores closer to my ear lobe, finally reaching this electric place and the question I had prepared and discarded, my full and complicated life and his responsibilities, are all irrelevant. The submerged workings of my subconscious have trickled into moonlight and swarmed my consciousness. There is no space left for denial. We are dangerous together and I can no longer summon any sensation of my wife's touch.

Rodney Wetherell

The Fort Macquarie Tram Depot

The romance of the old Sydney trams overshadowed everything
else in Dan's life: his job in a packing centre, his boxy flat in the
suburbs, his occasional entanglements with women. Compared
to all that, the trams were an unfailing combination of the reli-
able and the exciting. And they had to be 'old' and 'Sydney'.

Once he had ventured south to Melbourne at the urging of
other tram enthusiasts, but disliked the modern, fairly quiet,
vehicles in use there to this day. These could have been in
Brussels or Hamburg instead of an Australian city—and were
covered in high-gloss ads. Where were the rattlers, the old toast-
rack trams which took Dan back to the storied days when his
grandfather had driven them to Birchgrove, Coogee and Ryde?

The old man had told him about the conductors swinging
their way between compartments of the toast racks, which had
no central corridors; about paper boys hopping on and off; about
the loud, even raucous conversations among passengers, often
strangers to each other—not for them the sealed bubbles of the
phone-computer or the expressionless faces of the present-day
traveller.

The romance of the trams had a literal manifestation in
the lives of Dan's paternal grandparents, who had met on the
North Bondi line. His grandfather Ern used to say 'I picked
her up every day in the physical sense, but she picked me up
in the other sense'. He used to see a pretty young secretary

with untameable curls getting on in Bondi Road, and was delighted one day when she waved at him. He returned the wave of course, and this continued for a few weeks until she made a point of asking him some question about the tram service. Little exchanges followed, until one day she remained in the tram well after her stop, as far as the terminus where they had a longer talk. And the rest, they used to say, was history.

Older enthusiasts had told Dan of the thrill of travelling across the Harbour Bridge by tram—there had been nothing quite like it, not even a ferry trip. Someone kept a scrapbook of cuttings, describing all the arrests which had been made on Sydney trams, sometimes of major criminals—it gave Dan a kick to think of bank robbers and murderers travelling by tram. Then there were the 'characters'—not the famous Bea Miles who preferred to go by taxi, but plenty of others, from Domain speakers to poetry-spouting hoboes. He was not ashamed to admit, in tram-nut circles, that he dreamt about trams: of seducing a beautiful woman on a North Shore service, of meeting the Australian cricket team en route to the SCG, of angels travelling on the roof of an Earlwood tram.

Dan and his friends had been chuffed when they heard, a few years ago, that a new tram service would be established in Sydney—light rail, to be sure, only first cousin to a tram—and pleasantly surprised when it duly opened, running from Central Railway to Lilyfield. More lines were mooted, one to Dulwich Hill, and even one going straight down George St.

It was this last possibility that fuelled the notion that the old Fort Macquarie Tram Depot might be rebuilt. Dan's grandfather had said more than once that this had been, out of all the depots in the world, surely the most beautifully situated, on Bennelong Point between Circular Quay and Farm Cove.

From it, he said, coming as close to rhapsody as a working-class man from Arncliffe was likely to go, you got the perfect view of the Harbour Bridge, as well as Kirribilli with its two stone mansions, around to Cremorne Point, and then, as you turned, the wonder of the open harbour stretching to South Head.

Dan realized that the romance of the old Sydney trams had its touchstone, its epicentre, and what was left of its beating heart, in the depot demolished during the 1960s, after the last tram had reached its terminus. He realized that another building had been erected in place of the depot, and had even won architectural awards. However, he also knew that this building was considered far from satisfactory for its intended purposes. Surely, he told a gathering at the Tram Historical Museum, it would not be hard to have this other building demolished and the tram depot rebuilt. Only then would his great city truly come to life again.

Ali Jane Smith

Billycan

We had hoped the small museum would be air-conditioned. Historical alright, it turns out to be cooled by a couple of open windows and a pre-war fan. The sign 'farmhouse kitchen' points to a lean-to up the side of the house. A kookaburra stove, a meat safe, a butter churn, jelly moulds, nesting pudding basins. We're marvelling, 'Mum used to have one of those,' but the sight of my face in the back of an EPNS cake server is a reminder we're museum-pieces ourselves. Outdoors, a billycan suspended above cellophane flames. We always sat ours straight on the coals. As kids, we'd poke sticks in the fire, and watch Dad grasp the handle with a bit of rag. Then he'd stand well back and swing it over his head, making tea and a physics lesson. Seen enough, we're wondering out loud if there's a decent coffee within cooee.

Richard Holt

Bush Burial

Shovels | Oh yeah—I know what shovellin' sounds like | Three hours | crunch, scrape, flmp | Hutchy behind me mutterin', 'dig, bastard, dig' | An' now, this | An' this forever | He won't be happy | 'No-one 'll know,' 'e said | 'Nice and deep,' | 'Respectful, like…harder to find'

Cos 'e couldn't do nothing | I fucked up | What's a fella like Hutchy to do? | Sure I pleaded | Hutchy was cool | He listened to me | He heard me out | 'Hutchy, we're mates' | 'You an' me Hutch, you an' me'

How long's it been? | One year, ten, twenty | No more than that—old bones strong but no flesh | Ten I reckon | No memories, just…imprints | Cos there are things…like the roos | Thump, thump, thump, goin' down the hill | Thump, thump, thump, bouncin' up | No respect for the dead

An' cars on the road | They ain't never fixed it | Still bad like when me and Hutch came down | Everythin' shakin' and rattlin' | Gives me the tremors | So you get to know, but there's no time | No buildin' one moment on the last

The girl was a mistake | Made things messy | I felt her lying underneath me | Soft but cold she was | Cold like before | 'Cush' I called 'er | Eh Cush, how's it goin'? | Flesh turned to dirt | She's gone | I still think, though, sometimes | You an' me,

67

Cush…ya gotta laugh | She touched me once | A finger bone, maybe, slippin' around in the clay | How long? | A second, a day, a week, a year? | But she's not there now

But I do remember before | Like at school | Hutch was the one | Them teachers didn't stand a chance | —You, Hutchinson, and your mate, you'll never 'mount to nothin'— | They never seen the Bentleigh job | Hutch was brilliant | An' down at Wonthaggi that time, the bottlo | They never seen that

Oh yeah | We coulda done Parkville | It was all there | I remember | Had to hide out | Fine at first and then…cops everywhere | But Hutch was cool | No guns, nothin' | Knew them hills better than any of 'em | And then…the farmhouse in the valley | Food an' a car he says | The girl got in the way | I shouldn'a done it

Right here | Who could know? | Only Hutch | Hutch? | It's you | Ain't it? | Quiet | Nothin' | Restin' | Yeah—hard work diggin' | I remember | Three hours | Dig bastard dig | An' her all the while shakin' | An' you, Hutchy | Cool | Stop ya squirmin' | An' me never knowin' | An' thinkin' we'll be right with 'er out of the way | An' you shoutin' | Dig bastard dig

Hutchy? | Closer | How long's it been? | You came back Hutch | Careful now | Don't smash me up Hutch | Don't break me | Did ya know Hutch? | Still alive …the worst thing | An' her too, squirmin' | An' the big clods | An' the light goin' | An' air goin' | An' ribs cavin' in | An' taste an' smell | An' then…this | An' now…

…clods comin' off | weight coming off | like my ol' mum—I remember—liftin' the blankets | Peeling 'em one by one in winter

| Wake up fella…time fer breakfast | An' me under there, an' piss on the sheets an' Da' givin' me a hidin' an' yard-work for bein' trouble | Real close now…

Hang on, Hutch… | Someone's there | Rattlin' bones—cars 're comin' | You hav'n' got time | Quick | Ya gotta go | Hutch? | What 're ya doin'? | No Hutchy, don't mix us up, mate | Me an' her | I dunno… | Don' break us, mate | Careful Hutch

—Darryn James Hutchinson—

Eh?

—Darryn James Hutchinson? —

Coppers!

—Back off, Hutchinson | Put it down | Hutchinson | Put down the spade | Drop the bag. —

Floating

Crack | Revolver—one—two | Shotgun—three—four | Revolver—five—six—seven

Seven…bastards | Fallin'…fallin'…sack 'n all | An' 'er | An' you too | Crashin' down | You an' me Hutch | Together | Like ol' times | I knew it Hutch | An' me in the sack with 'er now | All mixed up | All fucked up

An' Dad in the backyard | Way back | Way back I remember | Dig, bastard, dig

Michael Sharkey

Stamina for endurance, endurance for economy

Stamina self-supporting trousers, made from guaranteed
Crusader cloth for the smart look men like. I'll bet. Featured
on the same page of the newspaper as the reported defeat of
a Bill to outlaw Communists, and the Government's rejection
of a share in the Anglo Iranian oil exploration in WA. The
Opposition noisy about the former, silent about the latter. I'll
bet. The politicians' photographs were half-tones, and the net
effect was grey. Like Stamina trousers: take your choice of grey.
In ancient times, the three sister-Fates were in the rag trade.
Clotho wove each stamen, plural stamina. Her sister goddess,
Atropos, cut each life's thread to the length their sister Lachesis
decided: made to measure. Sir likes grey? Stamina strides were
inflexible and almost indestructible: on warm days, hot and
clammy, eco-friendly to paspalum, double-cuffed to transport
burrs and accidentally dropped trey bits and zacs and cigarette
butts. In summer, they were portable saunas, generators of the
opposite mood to that of the smiling bloke in slacks and bomber
jacket in the advertiser's spiel. Ask anyone with a memory of
being a pimply wart who trudged dirt roads to a local school or
stumped along to a train and sweltered in a train and another
trudge to a public school or private college, dressed like every
adolescent male in the State, in Stamina slacks – the sweaty
regiment of the post-war, pre-wear what you like and who

cares generation. The Stamina company issued Men of Stamina cards to promote the brand. Chiang Kai Shek, a man of vigour, Christian by conviction, leading China on to freedom. Like the bloke in the bomber jacket, token of our parents' war and the one still running hot up Korea. Heart and soul of resistance, Chiang still fights on, tough as a bulldog, in no doubt of final victory. Men of stamina: Jan Paderewski, Garibaldi, Abraham Lincoln; the true-grit Britons: Ernest Shackleton, Disraeli; home-grown heroes: Edgeworth David, Douglas Mawson; Sir John Monash; rat-faced William Morris Hughes. And not one woman: Marlene Dietrich, Carole Lombard, Betty Grable, Rita Hayworth, Greta Garbo, Coco Chanel? Not to mention down-home local heroes raising kids as if production targets were the point until the revolution came? How the word is altered now. Type stamina in Google: sexual tips and hints for men. Maintain a longer erection and give women (note the plural) more pleasure in bed; how masturbation helps performance; change position, add brown sugar (weird); use secrets of perennial Chinese medicine; be an all-niter and make her scream. Who writes this copy? Women like only men with stamina. Ask anyone who went to school in the twenty years post-War what Stamina meant. Amazing feats of endurance? Yes, you'll bet. Who wore summer uniforms back then? Stamina always prickled, and sweat ran down in streams.

Monica Goldberg

A Leap of Faith

Faith: not wanting to know what is true.—Friedrich Nietzsche

Nineteen forty seven.

Was the year she arrived. The story goes. She went straight to work. On Kangaroos. Sewing patterns. In a small bedsit. Night and day. On the machine. To be honest. How. I am not really sure. Of the other gifts. That she made. There could have been sheep wool. Products. Koalas. In the corridor.

Perhaps. All I can say is that. She was a refugee. A shy one. That did her best. At the markets. Food. It was a blur. In the Kitchen. She was not Catholic. I can remember that. At least. She spoke. Yiddish. I can say for sure. There were also. Secrets. In the beetroot soup. Huge potatoes. At first. In the forest that is all she ate.

The truth was missing. Just vanished. I can remember the beautiful one. With the tail. On my shelf. It only had one eye. The ear had a big cut. The stuffing. Was falling. Everywhere. The remaining one. I can remember that. It had a quality. A glint. Even though it was never sewn. Up. The shape. It was so real.

Megan Marks

Cultural Exchange

The great Australian icon–the bum crack. I thought it was a global phenomenon, but it appears it is the great wondrous moment in Australia's history, where the arse-cleave is considered stylish. It seems Europe just hasn't taken it on as a fashion statement yet.

I was visiting family in the oh-so-dignified community of a small German town, a family event, when I was corrected on my 'kimme' as they call it. Corrected. How can you call it a correction when I was clearly exposing my proud Australian culture?

I'd been sitting with the oh-so-respectable aunties and uncles that were terrified of my lack of language, and probably of my comfort at the table. After minutes of silence and squirm, I thought it made sense to retire to the table of young-up-and-coming-respectables to see if I could stir some trouble. It seems I did.

As I departed the silence became a rumble, the dam had broken and word had got out – the colt from old regret had left the station, riding over the top of my squeezy hosen. Like Chinese whispers the tables passed the message around the room, until finally one of the up-and-comings did me the favour. 'Your bottom is out of your trouser.' And?

As every proud Aussie who has visited the northern hemisphere, I stood my ground. I was proud of where I came from, proud of our style, and proud of my credit-card-crack. It was a moment of no deliberation–it was family acceptance or national pride. I could stand the pride no longer and stood up, waving about delivering 'Aussie Aussie Aussie Oy Oy Oy' to a stunned and silent crowd.

I picked up my cardonnay, and retired to the doorway to have a smoke with the others that needed the escape of nicotine and freedom. They had missed the entire episode and welcomed me with open lighters. Between our few common words we established a camaraderie that only comes with defection and displacement. I'd found a niche where I could be respected for my culture and cigarettes.

And then someone dropped their lighter. As a proud Samaritan that likes nothing better than to help out mates, I bent over to retrieve it. I don't know whether it was the goodwill or the hosen slippage that created the gasps and guffaws, but suddenly I was on the other side again. The eyes flicked from person to person, me outside the circle. I thought stuff 'em and moved to the outer periphery, behind the cars, among the really happy folk–the drunk, the stoned and the homeless.

And that's where I found my folk, my calling. Among these people on the other side of the party hemisphere, the other side of the great cultural divide, I found my family. In true international style, they taught me every German swear word and indecency they could fathom, and I taught them about our misunderstood but proud Australian style.

And it didn't stop there. These people were fresh for ideas, children of enthusiasm, innovators of the first degree. They wanted to learn true Australian culture and to know what it felt to be Aussie. So it was in true Aussie spirit, true national pride, that I taught them the calling card of real Australiana. We snuck our way to the edge of the cars, in direct line of sight of the outside crowd, just within view of the inside crowd, hooted and wallowed, and dropped our duds.

Mark O'Flynn

Shoes

How graceful are your feet in sandals—Song of Songs

How graceful are your feet in thongs toying with the lesson of the beach. The sunburned footprints vanishing between sandcastle and tide. Someone rubs them dry with a towel. Examine every wrinkled toe curled under like a bootied infant's. Put them in your mouth, you know you want to, spit out the sand, centre of a chaotic assemblage. How graceful are your feet in Bata Scouts with laces you have learned to tie yourself, conjure the magic of those lovely knots. Toes scuffed on gravel, polished nightly with a brush reeking of dubbin. So shiny you can see the prefect's face reflected. Animal footprints like totems on the sole, a perfect record of the day's adventures in hardening mud, marching around the quadrangle to the brass of marching music, never missing a beat. How graceful are your feet in Brand-name runners dashing over fields of contest and fair play excelling at socialization—a gazelle, a cheetah, oblivious to the crippled fingers of the child labourer who contorted them from candle wax and logo. Go on, win that race, first prize for empathy. How graceful are your feet in steel-capped Blundstones carrying the nation from slag heap to prosperity. Kick them while they're down. Walk all over them. You know you want to. Your turn to get ahead. How graceful are your bunions, abrasions, ingrowths, the podiatrist's meal ticket. The foot-bound distortions of the toes stretching like cats when you wince in a fetish of sweat. Walk a mile in my shoes. How graceful the way you fling the bed socks to the corner like vanquished rags, exiled and separate, never to meet again. Take me to your hammock ravish my feet with oils and anointments. Whisper sweet nothings when I am too arthritic and fat, lean forward with the clippers. Do that for me my love. Then it's my turn. How graceful are your feet in fluffy slippers when you are withered and bent, the tide at last washed out, old soft shoe, heel-worn, shuffling in time with my shuffling.

Monica Goldberg

Not quite brilliant

The difference between false memories and true ones is the same as for jewels: it is always the false ones that look the most real, the most brilliant
—SALVADOR DALÍ

Life apparently.

At the railway. First. Cleaning carriages. It's true. They were refugees. Eastern. European tailors. At night they sewed. Bits of material together. Ladies' fashions. Sewn up. Pretty rough. At first. The cross. Area. In a one bed. Room flat. They worked hard. Semi-skilled. Could have been. The new Kangaroos. That made them. Enough money. For the jewellery boxes. Business. Not sure. All I remember. Is that they sparkled. Their Eye. Design work. Was unbelievable. Intricate. There were always samples. Lying. Around complicated. Musical things. Really. Very beautiful. Drawers and trays. I think. There were even secret compartments. The blue. Velvet was my favourite. Yet the red. Flocking. Was something special. The ballerina. On top. Never knew. People could order. Personalised ones. According to shape. Style and requirement. What I can say for sure. Is that they. Were not wooden. That was the main. Business that they did. Although. They couldn't speak. English or fill out. Forms or order things. At the dinner table. They looked. Normal. No one could see. Full time. Apparently. The Jewellery box. Business. It was quite successful. Eventually. Representatives. Went into the department stores. Luck. Then Grace. The brilliance. That was true.

Paul Mitchell

The Veteran

His burning frontline helmet shines, enemies fall into his long
smile; a flame turning yellow blue white burns the night alive; the
kid king of frontline boys; they throng him smoking, uniforms
slouch hats on blankets, stare at night-sky fireworks; pretty
crayon drawings explode, they sing Auld Lang Syne, but tanks
roll through heath, shoot fireballs from windmill guns and he's
a shield for his mates and he runs, stick in the air, shoots hail
into gods of thunder, and he's Yippee, a cowdie, from the silver-
screen; trees step back and hold each other; he whips his horse,
shouts, Carn he's a bushranger, his only weapon a stare; cocked
and aimed at trees that pull aside, plant themselves far from the
windstorm in his eyes; he rides wheatfields through towns, black
hair a dark star on a purple sky, he rides all night to the sea, at
dawn trots a ship's gangway; he sits on his horse on the boat,
circumnavigates Australia, bayonet drawn, his battalion roars
footballs at the sky, he scans for kamikazes, stares their grins
into the bellies of crowning whales; Jonah-mouthed he pulls his
ship by the reins, rides to the Wimmera, makes a fire, searches
the night for a hint of day, warms his hands, blisters tear his
palms away; he's an olive tree skinned by grizzly sun, sharp moon
carves him to a flower, hangs him from a branch; he's plucked,
dyed, worn by brides, strung to felt hats at wet cold weddings;
he sings in outdoor choirs, a soggy white and fallen flower. Trees

walk from mountains to meet at the creek, whisper nod bend conspire, then wave the wind away. They wade the creek, splash ring their trunks round his house, it sighs. A soft branch through a window strokes his forehead; the whisper of sweet songs from a night bird he'll never see. He wakes in his vinyl chair, shrinks and slides inside an empty beer bottle, bangs his fists on the glass; he's a tiny clown, a red smile up-side-down, then right-way-up; laughs crys laughs crys, pummels himself to make it stop but can't: the smile is him and he's the cry. His wife purple-eyed and Mary robed, his hands dig into her chest, her eyes the creek on a still fine day, and he bursts through her and into the sky; he's an airforce probe, picks up Wimmera war-wounded soldiers, drops them on the streets of Moscow, nineteen-fifty-five, under giant mushrooms he's in Russian uniform, a red star on his cap and a glint in his eye: behind his back, boxing kangaroo gloves have bayonets; he'll take the title from the Ruskies, the century will be his and ours, we'll be slaves to him, his kind, Anzac biscuit crumbs stuck for decades between our teeth.

Barnaby Smith

Whiteley's Blue

For years he had grandfather clocks for eyes, counting down to each decision over colour. A demand from his exalted other—a shock that shook the shock of curly hair that makes the city's emboldened savages obey. One day: swapping eerie dress codes with Scottish comedians. One day: frothing at the femininity of witches in murderous London. Always with head in hands (someone else's head) an apocalypse that brims with flow and heralds the greatest god masterpiece, brown veins, yet still just a symbol, and one for whom wearing scarves and cravats came so easily. Too easily. 'One day, child, you will produce a few strokes of meaning' with your charcoal from the shop, he says with those caffeinated chattering jawbones between periods of supernatural sober and an idea for a silk screen series.

The reality of every 'Australian' landscape changed upon looking, to buttocks. We render the terrifying spasms of flesh through sanctified light, the holy Monumental Glimpse always aroused, occasionally awry.

On the beach they are dissecting the nation, and nearby within the same white walls you, sir, used to transform, you are granting yourself the ultimate permission. Calling for help in the casual drift of a South Coast morning, Brett Whiteley is turning blue.

Elizabeth Hodgson

My 1960s

Your long driveway, your rose garden, your blank glass windows, the numbers you gave us—one to fifteen, your clothes, my red & white playsuit, your beds, your dolls, your books

the presents you gave—we never really owned, your big back yard, your swings, your monkey bars, your holidays, the beaches —where we swam each summer, your big-eyed cows, your milk, your chooks, your fresh eggs, your home-grown vegetables— boiled dry,

your bibles, your religion, your rules, your heaven, your hands, your anger—my hell, your locked cupboards, your locked rooms, your secrets, your presence, your large frame

—my tiny body, your hatred of self, your hatred of me, your justifications, your God, your God, your God—would never be mine. My life.

Charles D'Anastasi

travel

the mind would perk up at the sight of the word, the chorus of
its many voices. you sense how its jigsaws of nourishment would
position themselves. you're convinced, this time it's not a cheap
spin of fulfilment; even if, the mystery in the word might vaguely
unravel, along with the magic carpet, the unchecked promises,
the levitation you assured yourself is bound to happen, when
you leave the house to fend for itself for months on end, in dust
and silence, unanswered phones, books waiting. you arrive there,
of course—somewhere else; you always do—especially the other
you which follows you everywhere, where the world is a map
or another bottle of shampoo in equal measure. elsewhere, the
ocean sprawls and waits, and the blue you catalogued in a trance,
the one you got so close to, is also the one you will relinquish;
in spite of, all your plans, the whiff of anxiety in your desire,
the urgency to harness the ever changing light at the end of the
horizon.

Dael Allison

Margaret Olley sits for Ben Quilty

you think you've got it all and why not time's on your side. here
i am soft target skin the top of an old rice pudding lips puckered
apricots. the mouth's stubborn no denying. faces disintegrate
flowers shrivel why throw out them out before there's time for
gossip. is that look haunted depends on the romantic in you.
what about shrewd. eyeballing whatever's coming. it's coming
of course. he's good the kid guts and abandon plenty of paint.
understands gray like fairweather. mr always miss olley it was
always that. few blokes have got under my guard they've come
in hundreds to winkle me out. ark ark pass that little bottle. on
the moroccan table beside the cupid behind the chinoise fan.
anti depressants depressing taking them ark ark. another tablet
another smoke. this'll be a winner like bill there was a lovely man
nervy as a rabbit. blouson the french always have the word we
say blousey that australian nasal thing. blouson everything even
the hat gay abandon it was a celebration. all celebration looking
back. gave up drinking in '59 so i know my dates. been a gypsy
and here i am holed up in a hat factory. ark ark yes the ashtray.
look at him slapping paint around fierce clear enough who's
boss. body of colour that's how it is now impasto the texture of
lumpy custard better to stick to the face. orange highlight there
beside the eye and beneath the chin i've a wall of it nuanced

like watercolour otherwise it's dead. he knows. breaks it up to underglow keeps oodles of space fashionable i never wanted it. why not lug a wooden sheep around for years leave books open to whisper and murmur. life keeps crowding crowding in it's a process an accumulation. here's another visitor oh yes the artists are in the studio hurry hurry last days head left around the stuff no point leaning to the right. nail the window shut if you don't want people coming in two days without anyone is bliss but they keep coming. space can stretch it stretches to fit the mind's like that. by the grace of whatever gets the sun up in the morning.

Jude Bridge

Lamingtons

Cake Mistake?

Police raided another Country Women's Association clubhouse this morning. Five boxes of lamingtons and a Victoria Sponge were seized. CWA spokesperson Vi Williams, aka *Pikelets* Williams, said police had used excessive force, considering most of the ladies were having afternoon naps at the time. She also added that members of the CWA's North Dandaragan chapter had not been informed that sponge-based products had been added to the 'prohibited cakes and slices' list.

No arrests have been made. The raid may have been the result of an administrative error.

The Australiamerican Daily News, Thursday November 29, 2012

'Administrative error, my arse,' said Margaret. 'The government's been trying to close us down for years. And the press is just a sycophantic bulge in its pocket.'

The other ladies agreed. The September incident with the Carnakarra chapter of the CWA had been sensationalised by the same newspaper. A healthy discussion about fruitcake had been reported as 'an all out brawl between rival gangs'. The 'cake-stall bloodbath' in April referred to one of the trestle tables losing a plank and landing on Dot's foot. The injury had required a bandaid.

Polly asked timidly if she should put the kettle on. Vi rolled her eyes and put the whisky on the table.

'We're the last remnant of the Australian way of life,' Margaret continued, buttering a scone, '... apart from Indigenous people, and look what the government's done to them. So they're picking on us,' she said. 'Anyone not subsumed into the American culture, and I use that term loosely, is a goner.'

'Look at the other Aussie icons,' said Elsie. 'All gone, shot, made into purses for tourists, sold off or sold out. Kangaroos, koalas, Vegemite, Arnott's Biscuits, Peter Garrett ...'

Vi nodded, her head out of rhythm with her chins. 'My grand-daughter's been forced to drink Coke instead of homemade lemonade at school. Told to spell the word 'colour' without a 'u'. Forbidden to listen to Delta Goodrem. And they're planning an American military base next to the school. The Prime Minister has assured the Principal that noise will be limited and all fire will be friendly.'

Margaret snorted disgust. 'They want confrontation, we'll give them confrontation,' she said, passing the jam to Dot. 'Tomorrow, at dawn. My sources say there'll be another raid.'

'I've had enough,' said Polly. The other ladies were surprised. She'd always been a quiet little thing. 'My son's being followed to school, because I cook scones ...'

Vi stroked Polly's shoulder. 'It's not just about the food, Pol. We're too bloody Australian and too organised. The cops don't like the compound, the native garden, the verandah, the Blue Heelers, the smell of baking or the barbeque. Makes them nervous.'

'So, we're going down in a blaze of glory,' sang Polly.

'Or more likely, with a bullet in your back,' said Margaret.
'AC/DC rocks.'

'Long live Bon Scott,' shrieked Elsie.

'Long live Bon Scott,' the others echoed.

'Are we going to take hostages and shoot to kill?' asked Dot.

'You've been watching the Die Hard box set again?' admonished Margaret. 'I thought we'd thrown that out.'

Margaret explained that there were not going to be any shootings, hostagings, Taserings, torturings, grenadings or death-defying leaps from moving frypans.

The plan was to tell the police that this time, the CWA, North Dandaragan chapter, would not accept harassment of their members. They would cook sponge products of any description at whim, and would restore production of meatloaf immediately. They wished to be considered as a registered Australian Icon, by the Board of Australian Icons ...'

'I thought the Board had been disbanded,' said Polly.

'They kept it functional for Uluru and The Great Barrier Reef. Both are too big to move and too controversial to blow up,' said Margaret. 'Everyone get an early night. Vi will do the talking, if everyone agrees? She's the least likely to get angry. OK with everyone?'

The ladies concurred. Hot chocolate, made with a whisk and real chocolate, was prepared by Elsie.

Final Chapter for CWA

Twelve members of the North Dandaragan chapter of the Country Women's Association were gunned down by SAS soldiers in a dawn raid on the compound this morning. The Police Commissioner said that while the deaths were 'regrettable', the women were considered dangerous. It is alleged that the women were involved in money laundering, extortion and fraud. Margaret Smith, aka *Chutney* Smith, deceased, had been a person of interest to the police for months, thought to be involved in a 'revenge' killing of a member of the CWA's Bananabara chapter. The CWA is henceforth disbanded and outlawed.

The Australiamerican Daily News, Saturday December 1, 2012

This article was sponsored by the Coca-Cola Company

Caroline Reid

Who likes custard?

Donald Sutherland is watching me. He's got dandruff in his white Ned Kelly beard. He knows my birthday, says it's the same as his. He offers me a tic-tac. I take three. People come and go. He asks me what I like about trees.

'Their shade?' I say, squinting up at him.

He says he's been watching me for quite some time, from the library, behind green-tinted windows. Donald Sutherland in the Lilly Pilly Gully library, watching me watching him. Life's a funny thing.

Don and I walk for a while before we stop in the shade of a lilly pilly tree in the park. The playground is empty. He's been talking the whole time. Maybe that's his way of filling the emptiness. I smoke. Don talks about his wife, who is slowly going insane.

'We found out the day before Christmas,' he says. 'All the family were over. I said to my wife: Cry now. There there, dear, cry it all out.' The next day he woke early, before the fuss of Christmas morning had begun, children still dreaming of Santa and reindeer, not even the birds were up. The Don nursed his coffee and padded around the kitchen. The sky looked grey, diseased. He wished it over already. That was eight years ago.

I'm bored with Don's story now and wish he would go cry his blue eyes out somewhere else. In my mind I've already made him out to be more interesting than he is.

Later, I told Mick that Donald Sutherland breathed into my scarf, grabbed my arse with his grandfather hands, wrinkled but still strong and sexy, and we did it standing up, doggy style, in the park opposite the Lilly Pilly library.

Mick said, 'Who's Donald Sutherland?'

I tell Mick stories like this to make myself sound more interesting. We both know they're not true but I'm afraid if he really knows who I am he would leave. There's blandness in me. It's like badly made custard. Smoking helps. My mornings with Mick are coffee and toast and him wiping crumbs off the kitchen table. I like to shake cinnamon on the floor just to watch him sweep it up.

'Donald Sutherland is another way of saying cinnamon,' I said.

Cinnamon made me think of Baghdad in a fairy-tale, women selling brightly coloured scarves with gold trim, children stealing dates and dried fish, creating chaos.

As we ran out the door, down Paradise Road to catch the bus to work, I told Mick my great grandfather was an Afghani trader.

'This has got to stop,' he said, stopping abruptly. That's his way of making a point.

The B53 came and went.

'I like being late,' I said. 'Makes me feel like Jesse James, Steve McQueen. I think I'll photocopy my arse first thing when I get into work today.'

'This, this!' Mick waved his arms about. He looked like Buddy Holly in those glasses. 'No more Afghani traders, Steve McQueen! No more Donald Sutherland!'

I know what he means. It must get tiring. But he doesn't want the alternative, believe me. Bland custard? I don't think so. He has to trust me on this. Besides, he's got his sweeping, the Don's got his talking, and I swear to God that's Chris Walken waving to me from the back row of the cinema.

John Carey

Axel

I found the famous Melbourne underground artist, Axel *Chocka* Blok, nailing stray cats to the door of the Cathedral.

'I'm completing my thesis,' he explained.

'What course is that?' I asked and should have known better.

'Entrée,' he said.

We recorded the interview back at his place, a three-storey lifestyle apartment made over from a heritage incinerator.

I started with a leading question. 'How would you define outlaw art?'

'I don't need to,' he said, 'there's always blokes like you who'll do it for me.'

'Well, let me put it more simply,' I suggested. 'When you've tested the limits of transgression and pushed the envelope inside out, what will you find on the other side of the funhouse mirror?'

'Put simply,' he said, 'my exhibitions are curated by the Crown Prosecutor. I think I might nail you to the door of the Art Gallery.'

'I'll want a contract,' I demurred. 'Will I be a statement, a happening or a valuable artefact? There's a fee scale.'

'You'll be an Exhibit,' said Axel. 'Exhibit A: *The Hand That Feeds Me*. Exhibits have no rights. I do gratuitous crimes. Brace yourself.'

Charles D'Anastasi

after the votes are counted

in a country once blindingly imagined as the great south land,
a populist man, sleeps all curled up, foetus-like, with hundreds
of other men in a disused, large shed down on the wharf, close
to rows of silent ships, all primed for that arc of glory. when he
wakes up sometime during the night, to the sound of a tugboat's
foghorn, he discovers that all his brothers are only shadows of
strangers, which fills him with puzzlement and a heavy heart.
he stumbles into the night, cutting and wailing 'darkness is back
in town' 'darkness is back in town' darkness ...

Liam Copland

Top Floor Dogma

The magazine operates from the top floor. I tell people I work in the clouds, that things are different up there. I pack my lunch, screw on a tie, get a train and stand in a lift. As soon as I sit down at my desk, Kurt gets my attention by hissing from the cubicle over, and I close what I'm doing at my computer because office rumours are important for cohesion.

'Ed, you've seen the new guy?'

'The photog?'

'A real Bill Henson,' he whispers, smiling. 'I've heard rumours. Kiddy porn.'

'You probably shouldn't say that in here. Journalists work on this floor.'

Someone coughs and I try to work out if it's male or female.

'So what about him?' I ask Kurt, who is peering over the cubicle wall.

His eyes scan my space. He sniggers and says, 'He looks like the mannequin on the first aid poster.'

A few heads jolt up from their computers. Men and women. I hear the air conditioner move into its next phase. I recall an image of the new guy being escorted around by someone in reception, a tour of the top floor. I would describe him as rigid. But I can't tell how much of this summation is influenced by Kurt's words.

Only recently was the office adorned in precautionary posters. Laminated signage displaying first aid, the correct ways to sit at your desk, a map of places to assemble in the event of a fire, a blueprint of the office with safety zones marked in fluoro-green. I see people huddling in these zones, trembling. And then there's the extensive list of what constitutes workplace sexual harassment. Since its advent, men and women have never been the same, the binary never so apparent. Every man imagines women as glowing points of red—zones to avoid. Breathing near a woman can be enough.

I search for the first aid poster. I see it across the room and squint at it for a second. Its shiny surface makes it hard to focus on, but I see the flesh-coloured plastic mannequin and can't help smiling and nodding. 'Uncanny,' I say to Kurt, now searching for the new guy.

'If you're looking for him, he's at lunch. I know this because I've been watching him all day.'

'Creepy.'

'I agree. But we live by these signs now. Ever since management decided signage is important.'

'Your point?'

'Laminated law. I'm scared of women, in brackets scared of losing my job,' he says. 'By this logic, the new guy's a plastic mannequin. I wanna be consistent with my beliefs.'

*

I'm at the vending machine when the new guy lines up behind me. I can see him in the plastic door, standing in the rows of soft drink.

'Hello. You're Edward, the cartoonist,' he says.

Without turning around I examine him in the warped reflection. I nod and push a coin into the slit before reaching back into my pocket. I take my time. I scan his skin—his surface.

'How long have you been here at the magazine?' he says, monotonous. Is it monotonous? I wonder where the women are, if I'm safe here.

I'm searching for discolorations in flesh, sweat stains, eyebrows—human details. But the reflection is vague, he is vague, and I find myself searching for a crease, the point where two sheets of plastic come together. Kurt had said, 'Photographers are a bland people. That's why they're on that side of the lens.'

'Looks like we have to stick together,' he says, laughing. He can see my confused face in the reflection, and there's brief eye-contact. 'The men. The women. The rules.' He laughs again. 'It's a big joke, right?' More eye-contact.

I can tell he's becoming aggravated by my refusal to acknowledge him. I look away and push another coin into the slit. I have an image of a dark room, me naked and bound, him taking hurried photos. Kurt had called him a real Bill Henson. He'd also called him a mannequin, hadn't he?

'People say you're a real Bill Henson,' I say flatly, staring into his reflection.

I tell people I work in the clouds—a joke to fall back on at barbeques and bars. I tell them it's a different world, pieced together by things he said and she said.

'People say you're a mannequin,' I say, punching in the code for a Coke.

'People say you're lucky to still work here. People say you're the reason all these sexual harassment posters are up.'

Does he say this? Or is this what I expect him to say?

My can of Coke drops to the bottom of the machine and I turn around and touch the mannequin lightly on the cheek.

John Carey

Attack of the Killer Icons

Imagine being hit in mid-snorkel by a speeding truck with teeth...the nine lives of funnel-webs fifteen hours on the bottom of a swimming-pool or fifty minutes in a clothes-dryer clinging to a pair of smouldering knickers...a King Brown warming his long spine and bringing his root-canals to the boil on the bonnet of your limousine...old man croc barrelling through a sewer-grate spitting bones and backpacks...a slow smile for the honeymooners and a slow voice from Longreach via Alabama:

'Have a good one, do ya heah? Ay !'

Click go the shears, boys, click click click...cicadas swelling into the soundtrack as the sniffer-dogs paw at the ground...

In despair, you cling to a happy thought like a lifebuoy...but in the midst of life, there is a rusty stove chained to your leg.

Rodney Wetherell

The External Liaison Unit

'The password you put yesterday is not enough secure', said José minutes after his boss arrived at the office.

'Oh God, it's *Matilda* scrambled plus my birthday back to front—what could be less predictable than that?'

'You have used the same letters and digits from last time, with different scramble.'

'Oh, go scramble yourself!'

Until four months ago Alana had never worked in a unit of two, or one so secretive. She realized there was bound to be sparring between them, when they could not unload their work problems to any living soul outside the Unit. Only days earlier she had smelt dissension, when she saw José covering a piece of paper on his desk. On it she found a cartoon-like drawing of herself—it was unmistakable, and unflattering to say the least. Next to it were the words 'Level 4, legal'.

Alana Harbottle headed the newest and smallest unit within the ABC: the External Liaison Unit, consisting of herself and her assistant José Danielovic. It was also the least publicized, even among employees of the great national broadcaster on the same floor of the Ultimo building in Sydney. The title of the unit had been chosen as sufficiently dull to attract minimal attention to itself—people thought it was something to do with overseas program sales. In fact Alana's job was to sell not programs but program departments or units, to businesses either in Australia

100

or outside it, and in a matter of weeks she and José had notched up two such sales already.

'This week I want you to look at Archives, José. It might be boring, but the income stream you wouldn't believe—all those quaint clips from way back.'

'Yes, I would—it show on my screen last week only.' It was another thing about José that irritated her: he had always thought of it first. 'But next taxi for us should be food programs—celibate chefs, radio recipes, all like that. Big slice of cake!'

Alana gave this a big laugh. 'Yes, but we've been told not to attempt anything too diffuse at this stage. You'd have to divide foodie stuff into about ten and flog them off with different strategies.'

'OK, Archives—one big cake, one big buyer, all hushy-hushy.'

Another laugh as she said, 'Oh, go back to where you came from!'

'I am like little baby—don't know where I came from: Chile, Serbia? All gone, by earthquake, change of border.'

'I guess we're stuck with you.'

The principal problem for the ELU was its inability to advertise its products. You could hardly place an ad announcing *TV Drama Production Unit for sale! Creative and highly profitable outlet for suitable buyer!*—not when the present proprietor was a Government-funded body of noble public purpose. Privatization had arrived at the ABC much later than elsewhere, but was now in full swing, thanks to the ELU. The stock market reports had been first to go—a Chilean-Serbian initiative—then weather, in both radio and TV—a success for Alana.

'That lady Ma-Ma talked to me in the elevator yesterday—
she is Deputy MD, no?'

'Oh yes, Mary Mary quite contrary—a graduate of John
Howard's office.

And we say lift in this country.'

'She asked me if I remembered General Pinochet in Chile. I
say no, but my father worked for him.'

'Did he indeed? Was he…sympathetic to Pinochet?'

'Of course. He was businessman, and Pinochet asked him to
find sponsorship for some high military officers.'

'And did he?'

'I think so. I told Ma-Ma this.'

'You what? You must never put such ideas into the heads of
people like that. Any minute it will be policy in the ABC.'

'I think so.'

Alana walked away rapidly and found herself doing short
quick breaths as she took in what José had just told her. For
his work in the ELU, his closest model was his father selling
off military posts for General Pinochet! And he had told
the Deputy MD this with no reference to her. Suddenly she
understood the words next to his cartoon drawing of her: he
was about to organize the selling off of her position in ELU, no
doubt to Pinochet-type operators. If he succeeded, she would
probably hold her job, but would be working less for the ABC
than for a media business, possibly outside Australia! It could
be something very shady. Alana sat at her desk and began doing
a line drawing of her colleague, with his dark curls and flashing
eyes. Good-looking he may be, but he was a reptile in the grass.
Beside it she wrote 'Level 2, espionage background'. Alana made
herself a promise: to sell off José's position before he sold hers.

Kate Walter

Mutants and Missionaries

In the seconds before the machete blade severs my slim right wrist I think, Iggy was wrong; I can't stay whole in a city of mutants and missionaries.

*

I wake in the basement in the dark and reach out to touch my brother Isaac sleeping next to me. My hand lifts then falls softly onto the cold damp sheet. The moisture that drips from my ceiling to the slimy sandstone floor smells sulphurous. Grey light peeks through the grime on the only window; a single pane of Perspex marginally above the water line. During a storm I sleep in my dinghy.

I've been alone for a decade of my fifteen years. Isaac left just two years after the wave consumed the city and then sucked back, taking our parents with it. I don't remember the before-time, when this place was called Sydney. Pushing away the tattered oily blanket I dress myself in clothes that hide my intact frame, my unblemished skin, the venerated flesh that is my curse.

I skate the roof tops on a labyrinth of paths and bridges fashioned from debris and liberated building materials. You can cross Opera City this way, from building to building, over the choppy, dirty canals below. It's to avoid the missionaries. There's one on every pontoon, each vying to attract the vulnerable.

Those who have been driven mad with grief. Those who have lost more than me. They are many and growing.

The market is full, despite the early hour. People jostle for position to secure a meagre bunch of pale green seaweed. There's nothing else. Their skin is knotted and scarred, their sallow eyes shot with blood, the limbs they have left are mutilated and mangled. At the side of the market a hawker trades semi-smart prosthetics made from discarded dishwasher parts. Their electronics crackle and fuse in the red fog. I veer away and pull my hood down over my brow.

Ten minutes in I see it. A trader is harangued by man whose face looks like it has melted in the sun. His skin hangs in heavy jowls from his jaw, the red of his inner eyelids slack and infested with maggots. They're arguing over the cost of the swamp tobacco that's now unattended. I sidle in close and reach. A metal claw clamps around my right wrist. I try not to resist but it hurts. My captor is a woman, a trader from the next stall. Her nose is a cavernous hole. I can hear the air whistle through it deep into her lungs. She smells like rot.

'What are you up to?' Her voice thick like a clogged drain.

I pull away. My hood drops back. Shocked, she drops my wrist and hisses, crossing her chest with her claw. She says only one word: *Whole*. The crowd is silenced, caught by surprise, then they press against me, jostling for a look. Their cries ripple, from urgent whispers to incredulous wails that combine to a chant: *Whole, whole, whole*. I shove my way to the edge of the market, pressing through my panic against the flesh and fake limbs that are craving to touch me.

Iggy sucks gratefully from a joint dangling from his fat bottom lip, the paper soggy with saliva. I can't stand the stuff; the mustard yellow smoke smells like possum crap.

'Don't mention it,' I say.

He looks at me, the jowls on his mangled face quivering. We're sitting high on The Bridge, our legs dangling into space and skateboards wedged safely behind us. The wind buffets us in strong short gusts.

He raises his hand in protest, his two fingers stiff and scabby. 'You're crazy.'

'I've made up my mind'.

'I won't let you,' Iggy says. 'That's the thing.'

'It's not your decision to make.'

I know that Iggy holds sway over the mutants who occupy the old Opera House. And he owes me. I stand and grab my board.

'Tell them I'll give them anything they want,' I say.

He nods, watching as I climb down to my dinghy below.

*

We're inside the concert hall on a mezzanine before a giant organ. Wind whirls into its pipes like whale song. My heart quickens.

A fire burns in an ancient petrol can, a baby bat skewered above. Its singed fur smells like kerosene. Grey water whirlpools in the auditorium below, thick with trash and debris from the surrounding sea. The building creaks as waves break against the outer walls. I'm stretched over a dais, staring up at the thousands of dried body parts that are strung from the ceiling above me. A man with a glass eye and breath like faeces pins me down with one hand and raises his machete with the other.

The pain is exquisite.

Biographies

In 2012 Dael Allison completed her Masters in Creative Arts, UTS, based on the artist Ian Fairweather, and launched her second volume of poetry, *Fairweather's Raft* (Walleah Press). She currently lives in Kiribati, central Pacific.

Jude Aquilina has published four collections of poetry, including *Knifing the Ice* and *WomanSpeak*. She lives on a walnut farm in the Adelaide Hills and teaches creative writing at TAFE.

Jude Bridge's short stories have appeared in *indigo*, *dotdotdash*, *The Big Issue Fiction Edition 2012*, *that's life*, *Sand Journal*, *The Fish Anthology* and online with Headspring Press.

John Carey is an ex-teacher of French and Latin and a former actor. His fourth poetry collection, *One Lip Smacking* (Picaro Press) will appear in March 2013.

Julie Chevalier writes poetry and short fiction in Sydney. She has written *Permission to Lie* (Spineless Wonders) and *linen tough as history* (Puncher & Wattmann). *Darger: his girls* (P&W) won the Alec Bolton Prize. juliechevalier.net

Pawel Cholewa, 25, lives in Melbourne and works as a secondary school teacher, plays in a band, studies, travels often and writes whenever possible.

Liam Copland's writing has been described as bizarre, his fast-paced style both humorous and deeply moving, and his dry Australian realism laced with a colourful surrealism—a fresh and exciting execution.

Moya Costello is a lecturer in Writing, School of Arts and Social Sciences, Southern Cross University, with three books published. Recent creative work is in the journal *Etchings* (with Patricia Costello) and the anthology *Small Wonder*.

Charles D'Anastasi is a Melbourne poet. He has been published in various journals and anthologies. His chapbook *The unreliable harbour* was published by Melbourne Poets Union.

Zoe Annabel Davies is a writer from Melbourne. Despite volunteering at SYN.FM as Arts and Entertainment Manager while completing her university degree she always finds time to people watch. Zoe contributes to *Alphabet Pony* and has had her photography published in *Visible Ink*.

Trina Denner lives, loves and writes in Brisbane. She holds a Masters Degree in Writing and is currently engaged in a PhD project exploring Young Adult fiction.

Linda Godfrey is an editor and publicist for Spineless Wonders and hosts the South Coast NSW poetry event, Rocket Readings. She holds a Masters in Professional Writing (University of Technology, Sydney) and can't resist a prose poem.

Monica Goldberg is a surrealist writer and artist. She has taught writing in community centres and has worked as a photographer. Her first novel is about the significance of cryptic faith.

Stu Hatton is a Melbourne-based poet and editor. He teaches within the School of Communication and Creative Arts at Deakin University. Recently his poems have appeared in *Cordite, fourW* and *The Best Australian Poems 2012*.

Tim Heffernan was born in Hay, NSW. He has published poems in *Cordite, Thylazine, Eureka Street, Blackmail Press*, the Red Room Company's *Disappearing* and the *Wagga Wagga Daily Advertiser*. He lives in Wollongong.

Hilary Hewitt lives and works in Sydney's inner west where she writes poetry and prose. She was short-listed in 2012 for the inaugural Overland Victorian University Short Story Prize for New and Emerging Writers.

Elizabeth Hodgson is a Wiradjuri woman. She won the David Unaipon Award for her collection *Skin Painting*. She is working on a collection of poems based on the reasons for her disastrous love life.

Richard Holt first wrote very short stories to incorporate in artworks but gave up painting and now blogs fiction and verse about love and other nonsense at smallstoriesaboutlove. wordpress.com.

Carol Jenkins' first book of poetry, *Fishing in the Devonian* (Puncher & Wattmann, 2008) was short-listed for the 2009 Victorian Premier's Literary Awards. Her second book, X^n, will be released early in 2013.

Anna Kerdijk Nicholson's second book, *Possession*, received the 2010 Victorian Premier's Prize and Wesley Michel Wright Prize. In 2011 it was shortlisted for the ACT Judith Wright Prize and the NSW Premier's Prize for poetry.

Paul Kew currently resides on the south coast of NSW where he is working on his writing.

Peter Lach-Newinsky has won the Vera Newsome Prize and the MPU prize twice. Poetry books: *The Post-Man Letters* (Picaro 2010), *Requiem* (Picaro 2012), *Cut a Long Story Short* (Puncher & Wattman, forthcoming). He works a small permaculture farm near Bundanoon, NSW.

Jessica McLean writes stories taken from life, in multiple modes, accessible on twitter @jess_emma_mc. She is finishing her first novel, *Smiling at Crocodiles*—a tale of love and loss and the journeys in between.

Megan Marks is a jack-of-all trades, mistress of one—the ability to be filthy in any situation. This was one such opportunity. She hopes her mother is rolling over in her grave.

Bronwyn Mehan lives in Sydney. Her fiction and poetry have appeared in *The Age, Island, Meanjin, Southerly* and *Best Australian Poems 2012*. She is the founder of Spineless Wonders.

Paul Mitchell has published a short story collection, *Dodging the Bull* (Wakefield Press) and two collections of poetry, *Awake Despite the Hour* (Five Islands Press) and *Minorphysics* (IP). paul-mitchell.com.au

jenni nixon is a Sydney poet and performer. Her publications include *Café Boogie* and *Agenda!* Her poems appear in *Best Australian Poems 2009 and 2010* (Black Ink), *Harbour City Poems* (Puncher & Wattman) and *Seeking the Sun* (Central Coast Poets 2012).

Mark O'Flynn has recently published a comic memoir, *False Start*, and the novel, *The Forgotten World*. His fourth collection of poetry was *Untested Cures*. In 2012 he came second in the Newcastle Poetry Prize.

Jeremy Page has recently completed a BA in Sydney, majoring in Writing and Philosophy. Also a professional graphic designer, his ambition is to eventually write, design and publish his own poetry and short fiction.

Sylvia Petter is an Australian writer based in Vienna, Austria. She is the author of the collections, *The Past Present* (2001), *Back Burning* (2007) and *Mercury Blobs* (forthcoming in 2013). She is currently revising a novel.

Caroline Reid's plays have been performed and published, as have her stories. She's finishing off a first collection, *Satisfied*, and curates Spineless Wonders Presents ... a short evening of tall stories at Adelaide's Wheatsheaf Hotel. carolinereidwrites. blogspot.com.au

Michael Sharkey's poetry collection, *Another Fine Morning in Paradise* and biographical work, *Apollo in George Street: The Life of David McKee Wright* were published in 2012. He reviews poetry for New Zealand and Australian publications.

Ali Jane Smith's poetry collection, *Gala* was published in 2006 as part of the Five Islands Press New Poets Program. She has been the recipient of a Longlines Residency for Regional Writers at Varuna–the Writers House.

Barnaby Smith is a writer, poet and musician based in Sydney. His work has appeared in *Best Australian Poems 2012*, *Southerly*, *Wet Ink* and *Regime*. He also writes for *Rolling Stone*, *ABC Arts* and *The Quietus*.

Barrie Walsh, a fruitpicker in Griffith NSW, is currently writing a collection of short stories and a few poems under the working title *Noctural U-Turn Suite* (*NUTS*).

Kate Walter is a student of Creative Writing at the University of Sydney. She loves writing screenplays. Her short story *Disembodied* appeared in *Short and Twisted* (Celapene Press 2011).

Lynette Washington is a PhD candidate in the Creative Writing program at the University of Adelaide where she is studying short stories and digital publishing. 'The Swarm' is her first published story.

Rodney Wetherell worked for many years in ABC Radio Drama and Features, where he was an editor and producer. His writing includes radio features, articles and (so far unpublished) novels.

Also from Spineless Wonders

A treasure trove of writing from some of the most innovative practitioners of prose poetry and microfiction in Australia.
KABITA DHARA, EDITOR, READINGS MONTHLY

Small Wonder
prose poems & microfiction

edited by Linda Godfrey and Julie Chevalier

Here are short and clever pieces by thirty contemporary Australian writers on the eroticism of mashed potato, parenting as magic realism and a tongue-in-cheek history of the Cyclops bicycle. Includes award-winning writers Michael Farrell, Keri Glastonbury, Judith Beveridge and Peter Boyle. Features prose poems and microfiction selected by competition judge joanne burns.

Contains illustrations by talented young artist, Paden Hunter.

*Quality short Australian fiction, packed with surprises. Prepare to
be transported.* MARION HALLIGAN

Escape
Anthology of short stories

edited by Bronwyn Mehan

ESCAPE has unexpected tales of contemporary life,
comedy, tragedy, mystery, romance, sci-fi, dystopian
fantasy, a homage to David Foster Wallace and lots more. .
Features award-winning writers such as Ryan O'Neill, Jen
Mills, Andy Kissane, Louise Swinn, Julie Chevalier, A.S.
Patrić and Kim Westwood, as well as stories chosen by Sophie
Cunningham in the inaugural Carmel Bird Short Fiction
Award.

Contains illustrations by talented young artist, Paden Hunter.

Unflinching realism … compelling and complex in equal measure.

Permission to Lie

by Julie Chevalier

In this wonderfully diverse collection, Chevalier does not flinch from delving into some of the messier aspects of contemporary Australian culture, whether inside prisons, nudist camps or in cut-throat boardrooms. Cover art and six pages of quirky illustrations by Paden Hunter.

> *'Holding together the extensive range of this collection is prose of a deceptive simplicity, taut, droll, hinting at greater depths, never giving too much away. A new voice in Australian fiction, wry, gritty, knowing and true.'*

Fiona McGregor
author of ***Indelible Ink***

Strange and often unsettling stories ... a fresh and vibrant new voice. Bookseller + Publisher

The Rattler
& other stories

by A.S. Patrić

This entertaining collection set in and around contemporary Melbourne. Sometimes serious, sometimes seriously playful—always written in breathtakingly beautiful prose. Cover art and illustrations by Miles Allinson.

> *'An explosive mix of muscular prose and sharp originality. In this collection, A.S. Patric proves himself to be a writer who must be taken very seriously.'*

Vanessa Gebbie
UK author of ***Short Circuit, A Guide to the Art of the Short Story***

Newton-John, who wields a superb descriptive talent.

Fault Lines

by Pierz Newton-John

Seamless prose, undercurrents of contemporary music, the urbane writing, the suburban settings, but it is all happening behind closed doors.

Here are the fault lines in all our lives, and Newton-John, with an unflinching eye and a mesmerising style, lays them bare in this sequence of expertly crafted vignettes. Fault Lines returns the grit to the Australian literary landscape.'

Matthew Condon
author of **Trout Opera**

Damaged In Transit

by Mary Manning

Seamless prose, undercurrents of contemporary music, the urbane writing, the suburban settings, but it is all happening behind closed doors.

Seventeen short stories about travels of various kinds add up to a very coherent collection that sets up little echoes and contrasts from story to story. Manning has an original, confident style and a sharp eye for the weaknesses and idiosyncracies of human nature.

'An intelligent, engagingly written and thought-provoking work...absorbing.' DR BRONWEN LEVY

Lives of the Dead
& other stories

by Jane Skelton

Jane Skelton writes cool prose about hot landscapes, about characters seeking relief from strong emotions, about characters whose lives are tied up, inextricably, with the Australian landscape.

'Jane Skelton shows a fine literary talent.'
HELEN BARNES-BULLEY,
Literary Program Manager, VARUNA.

EARWORMS
short Australian audio

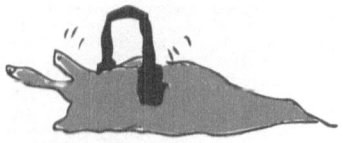

Stories that stay with you

Earworms are those songs with unforgettable hooks that get stuck in your head but Spineless Wonders brings you short Australian earworms—stories by award-winning writers that you definitely won't want to forget.

Stuck in a queue? Don't stress. You can listen to our selection of funny, political and thought-provoking prose poems and microfiction from our anthology, *Small Wonder*.

Got a pile of washing-up or ironing to do? Housework's not a chore when you can listen to short fiction from our anthology, *Escape*.

Commuting every day? Traffic jams are not a problem when you can listen to the latest in contemporary short fiction from Spineless Wonders.

Prices range from $0.99 to $2.99. Gift vouchers available.

Listen to our audio trailers now at
www.shortaustralianstories.com.au.

Spineless Wonders publications are available in print and digital format from participating bookshops and online. For further information about where to purchase our print, audio and ebooks, go to the Spineless Wonders website:

www.shortaustralianstories.com.au